Perry Normal and the Mystery of Lost Atlantis

Book 3 in the Perry Normal Adventures

I0601900

Mason Stone

For all who know, deep down, it
is waiting for us.
And for my Pig, who knows
more than anybody.

Revised edition.
© 2019 Red Pine Publishing,
Toronto, Ontario M6C 1L3
Canada

Contents

Act I The Deep Blue

Chapter One   The Water Out There

Off the starboard side of the boat, Perry Normal could see straight down into the deep blue water. He was a mile offshore from Ft. Lauderdale, and the Atlantic was already over 200 feet deep beneath him.

He struggled into his tank and fitted his mouthpiece, then his mask and his fins.

"Let's go over the side, people. Alternate! Port—then starboard, until everyone is in the water."

The dive captain and owner of Key Largo Dive Club—Darius Frame—was strong, ambitious, and cunning. Perry would know this much later.

At eleven years old, Perry was a typical 7th Grade middle school student, better than most at understanding Science, his passion in life.

This was his first trip to sunny Florida and the first time he tried scuba diving outside of a swimming pool.

Perry had no preconceptions about his summer vacation with his parents; whatever happened—if it was interesting, was fine with him.

Anyhow, he had a way of attracting mysteries and strange circumstances, as if the Universe were playing games with him, teasing him to find the solution to the riddles he was presented with.

The sensation of floating, weightlessness, was unreal, Perry was thinking. All the colors of the fish; even the dangerous moray eels were colored differently, and all were cranky in the presence of human invaders.

The sandy bottom was where the circle of newbies gathered and practiced hand signals and checked the pressure in their ears. Even in 25 feet of water, the pressure increased noticeably, and required a simple procedure to equalize it.

Altogether there were about ten in their little party, kneeling on the sea floor, letting the Gulf Stream flow past them on its journey north and east to Europe.

The first rule, Perry had learned, is to dive with a buddy. Always have someone to monitor your situation, as this underwater world was strange and often hostile to visitors.
They had practiced sharing air in case one buddy ran out down there. Safety first, the dive

instructors always said. In open water, it was clear why.

This first real dive in the real sea was an eye-opener for all the students. It was also thrilling, and opened new possibilities for enjoying the friendly Florida community of beach and water lovers. Perry wished Henry were here. Then he would have a for-real partner, not just a temporarily-assigned swim buddy.

After they surfaced, and went ashore for lunch, Darius revealed a reason why he was such an avid diver—treasure!

Spanish galleons loaded with gold and precious stones such as emerald had been wrecked on both coasts of Florida—the Gulf of Mexico side on the west, all the way down to the Florida Keys, and on the east coast from north of Miami all the way to St. Augustine.

The storms were terrible at times in these waters, and dangerous reefs and shoals surrounded small cays and islands that ripped the bottom of a ship's hull open like a garbage bag, spilling men and cargo into a watery void. The great wood sailing vessels of the 1500s and 1600s were no match for the fury of the Caribbean weather.

And of course, there were the buccaneers—'pirates' people know them as today. They would steal and plunder anything of value and burn or blast their victims into matchsticks, and these unlucky ships and cargo lay on the bottom, many fathoms below.

Darius stood on the deck in brilliant sunshine.

"I can tell you that there are undiscovered wrecks all up and down the coast, just waiting to be found, and salvaged. Doesn't that make our classes a lot more exciting?"

Everyone murmured in agreement.

"What if we do find treasure? Can we keep it?" asked Santiago, a student from Mexico.

Of course, as I have a license to find, explore, and recover artifacts from offshore wrecks in American waters. And beyond, in the deep blue, the traditional rule for mariners and salvors is— finders, keepers. You follow me?"

"When can we start hunting?" several said in quick succession.

"Once we finish our course and get certified," Darius said. "Tomorrow we dive a reef and its tricky currents and tidal surges. That will be a vital step in our open-water training."

"Are we ready for that?" whispered Amy, a freshman at Florida State, diving for the first time with a tank and gear.

"*He* obviously thinks so," said Ted, an older boy in grad school in Virginia.

They looked at Perry.

"How do you feel about it? What's your name? Perry?" Ted was tall and strong and gave an air of confidence that the crew needed about now.

"I don't know," Perry said. "I'm just taking it one step at a time."

Survival at sea is a combination of skill and quick thinking. All the students had scary scenarios in the back of their minds: shark attacks, getting lost or disoriented, running out of air, anything that old movies might have used to scare moviegoers in the name of entertainment.

Only this time, they weren't in a movie theatre. Bare legs and arms looked deathly pale and flimsy underwater. And maybe tasty to certain hungry species waiting for a meal.

Tomorrow would give them another chance to find out.

***

This all started when Robert and Lisa Normal decided Florida was where their holiday should be. Lots and lots of sunshine, amazing beaches and tourist sites. They were clear that they needed a good long break from work. The school break was at least eight weeks and Perry would go with them for sure.

Gabby missed getting a credit in Biology and would take summer school in July to make it up. She would stay home. She certainly was old enough, she had a driving license, and even a boyfriend.
If things worked out, she could fly down later.

"Hey, can I learn to scuba dive this summer?" Perry was asking.

"That's a good idea," his Dad said. "This is a life skill."
Perry's parents were always concerned that their kids have 'life skills', which included interesting hobbies and recreational activities that would expose them to new experiences.
Perry was fortunate to have parents who were both open-minded enough to permit them to do new things, and wealthy enough to pay for it.

"Why don't you Google a couple of dive clubs that train new students, using certified instructors and proper equipment."
"Sure, Dad, thanks!"

Perry found out that water sports in a place like Florida were extremely popular with both locals and tourists. With its long white-sandy beaches and numerous boating marinas, Lauderdale was an excellent place to start an exciting new activity. He jotted down the names of a couple of likely places to learn underwater training out of Ft. Lauderdale.

His parents preferred to stay ashore in their luxury hotel, and instead of hanging out on the beach all the time, they could visit the antique and art museums, and just wander on Las Olas Boulevard with a cappuccino and croissant in their hands.
Which is pretty much what most adults want on a holiday. No stress— no problem!

Their hotel had a huge pool, with beach furniture and umbrellas right on the deck.

Weird how grown-ups pay big bucks to stay at a beach resort, but won't go swim in the ocean. They prefer the pool, where everything is clean and tidy, and waiters in fancy outfits wait on you, 'hand and foot', as Perry's Dad liked to say. 'Service is everything,' he often said.

Perry, however, wanted to taste the saltwater, see the fish up close, maybe a shark, and be literally immersed in the whole scuba thing. This was his chance, and he was going to take it!

"Wish you could come down, Henry." Perry texted his best friend, Henry Gerrit Schuyler, who was also a resident Science geek at Brackendale Middle School.

They had lots of adventures together. Like the time last year when they 'borrowed' the Science Dept. telescope for a little home viewing—without permission of course.[1]

And the time when Perry disappeared for a few days after constructing a simple model of a wormhole, that turned out to be a fairly accurate representation, which led to a mysterious event that proved Time Travel is real. That's what Perry says, anyway.[2]

"I have to convince my parents. Hey, Perry! Why doesn't my Mom talk to your Mom, and maybe they will agree? Leave it with me. I will get back to you."

Henry did. "My Mom wants to know the name of the hotel where you are staying. I think they just woke up out of their daydream of having a barbecue summer when I suggested Florida. Let me know."

Later Henry texted: "Okay, Perry. This is coming together really nicely. My parents have booked a luxury room in the same hotel you guys are in,

---

[1] Perry Normal and The Moons of Saturn
[2] Perry Normal and The Time-Slips

and we will be flying down day after tomorrow. I can't wait. We are gonna have an awesome time."

Perry texted back: "Tell them to sign you up with Key Largo Dive Club—it's in Ft. Lauderdale, not Key Largo, actually. They have intro classes for complete newcomers. You don't even have to know how to swim that well. Basic qualification: tread water for, like, five minutes!"

"I'm in. Gosh! I don't even have a swimsuit," Henry noted.

"Put it on the list, my boy. We are going to wear it out this summer!"

Perry was delighted that he would have his pal Henry to share whatever adventures they would get into. It is so much better when there are two of you.

***

Henry arrived when he said he would.

Henry's parents did not know the Normals all that well, but sitting around a lovely pool on a 'gorgeous' day (that's what his Mom called it) was enough to make them friends from the get-go.

Henry's Dad was an electrical engineer, and Perry's Dad was an accountant, but, after a few beers, and big screen TV with Major League

Baseball right behind the pool deck in the bar, they acted like they had known each other for years.

Perry and Henry had another idea.

They wanted to know more about the pirate treasure that Darius Frame was interested in finding.
The library was an old Colonial-style mansion that had been restored and upgraded. They not only had super-fast Internet, they had old books and maps that focused on wreck diving on both coasts of Florida, right down to the Florida Keys—where 80% of the Spanish gold had been recovered.

The boys pored over books all afternoon. They found all kinds of information, some of it historical, some of it geographical.

"Do they have volcanoes down here?" asked Henry.
Volcanoes were his specialty; he knew everything—I mean everything about volcanoes, and tectonics, and earthquakes and their origins. He could've taught college classes, even though he was only eleven, he knew so much.

"No, I don't think so, Henry," replied Perry.

"But they have The Bermuda Triangle!" Henry said excitedly.

"That's a whole other thing," said Perry. "Probably caused a few shipwrecks though."[3]

The boys were daydreaming all their childhood fantasies, like being a real pirate, or diving on a wreck full of treasure, or proving that The Bermuda Triangle was real, and really did cause airplanes and ships to disappear forever.

Perry was on the computer.

"Hey, Henry. Look at this. Have you ever heard of the Lost Kingdom of Atlantis?"

"Sure, Perry. And it's the lost *city* of Atlantis. It's, like, legendary since the Greeks first wrote about it. Plato, actually. He said he got the story from a wise man in Egypt. I wonder where the Egyptians got the story?"

"Some divers claimed to have found evidence of lost Atlantis off the shore of Florida, and the Bahamas. Like, suspicious looking ruins."

"Nobody knows, number one, if Atlantis even existed, and number two, where it was, exactly." Henry said.

---

[3] The Pirate Curse

But they worked like a team—Perry browsing the Internet, and Henry browsing the bookshelves.

"Boys, the Library will close in ten minutes, so you need to logoff, and put any materials on the cart here." The librarian was an elderly lady with a friendly smile.

"Hey, Perry," Henry whispered. "Doesn't she remind you of Miss Floon-- our school librarian? They are both old enough to be categorized as 'dinosaurs'."

"Shhh...she will hear us," Perry said, laughing into his armpit.

They resolved to return tomorrow to continue their investigation of lost Atlantis.

First and foremost, they had to decide whether it extended across the Atlantic Ocean from the coast of Spain, and could have existed in the waters off this part of Florida.

***

"Where are you boys going in such a hurry? Diving lesson?"

Mr. Normal and Mr. Schuyler were drinking coffee at the bar, and later would be drinking something alcoholic at the same bar. Grown-ups. So predictable. So boring.

"To the Library. We're doing some research on Atlantis, Dad," said Henry.

"Oh yeah. Some people think it was near here, maybe the Bahamas were part of the island that was destroyed by a volcano in one terrible night."

"Really?" said Henry.

"Just like Santorini," said Perry. He shuddered, as if a sudden chill hit him.[4]

"Yeah, that's right. In fact, some people believe that Santorini was the original source for the legend that Atlantis was blown away in a single cataclysm," Henry's Dad said.

"How come you know so much about this Dad?" Henry inquired.

Henry's Dad replied: "I was interested in the legends myself when I was your age. Hey! If you boys are going diving out over The Continental Shelf, why not keep your eyes open for, you know, ruins or temples—stuff like that!"

The boys learned in Geography that, just offshore on both oceans, is a broad, shallow slope called the Continental Shelf.

---

[4] See: Perry Normal & The Time-Slips

It was probably dry land at one time, but when the great ice-sheets in North America and Europe melted, about 10,000 years ago, the sea level rose and drowned coastal villages and towns forever. England lost a whole mysterious kingdom called Lyonesse.

Perry knew this, and so did Henry. But a trip to the library would refresh their memory and give them new leads.
Was Lyonesse another name for mysterious Atlantis? wondered Henry. *Maybe.*

***

The library was open. The boys raced to the work desk area. Each occupied a carrel.

Soon they had a pile of books about this topic of Atlantis, including some unusual titles like 'The Devil's Sea' and 'Edgar Cayce on Atlantis'.
Edgar Cayce, they discovered, was a famous American psychic who not only acknowledged Atlantis as a real kingdom in very ancient times, but predicted it would rise from the waves again—here! Off the Florida Coast!

That would be so cool! The boys were in agreement on that point.

What they also discovered is that books are long on talk, but short on evidence.

"That brings us back to what your Dad said, Henry."

"What's that?"

"There has to be physical, archaeological evidence brought to the surface—assuming Atlantis is underwater, as most people think. I mean, coins, cups, pieces of masonry—stuff that can be studied and verified by experts."

"That means somebody had to be looking. Maybe, while we're looking for Spanish or pirate gold, we might find something, Perry. Something really significant."

"You're thinking the same thing I'm thinking, Henry. Like always. Two great minds in sync." Perry was grinning and slapping Henry on the back.

"Let's get to the dive school, Henry. The second class starts in an hour. Our quest lies at the bottom of the sea, Henry. Let us venture forth!"

Chapter Two   Getting Deeper

Key Largo Dive Club kept its dive boat at the marina at the mouth of the Intracoastal Waterway--hundreds of miles of canals and moorings that gave sport boaters of every kind virtually unlimited access to the Atlantic Ocean over the Continental Shelf, that ran for a hundred miles or more offshore, into the deeps.

That much the boys could see on Google Earth. And on any of the maps they were collecting at the local tourist information center.

Florida was a paradise for boaters and beach lovers. Now Perry understood why his parents chose it--instead of, say--Europe.

Perry and Henry arrived at the community center whose pool was the focus of today's lesson.
    "Hi, Perry!" said Amy. "Ready for some more technique?"
    "For sure! Meet my best pal, Henry."
    "Hi, Henry," said Amy.
Santiago shook everybody's hands.
    "Hola, amigos! What a great day!"

Henry and Perry go changed into swimsuits, as the lessons today were going to focus on basic swimming skills.
    "Just tread water, Henry. Simple."

"What's 'tread water' mean? Like pretend you're walking while floating?"

"Here comes Darius; he'll show you...us. I'm no expert, for sure."

The twins—Yasmin and Fatima—newly immigrated and still quite shy, were already in the pool. They were pretty good swimmers, thought Perry.

"Gather round, people," shouted Darius, waving his hands in a sweeping motion.

"OK. Today let's work on basic survival swimming: treading water, and drown proofing. Everybody get a buddy. Most of you have one by now."

Henry and Perry were tall enough to stand in the shallow end.

There were ten of them—so Courtney paired up with Marie from Montreal, and invited Santiago to be the third in the 'pair'.

"The secret to treading water is to relax," said Darius. "You waste precious energy by being stiff and rigid." He went around the pool to each pair, and corrected them where necessary.

Jacklyn was a local, married, on a brief getaway from her job, and she was paired with Sandy, who looked slightly overweight, and rather nervous about being in the water.

Darius spoke in a quiet tone to her, assuring her that everyone who takes his classes loosens up and gets how to do it, no problem. That seemed to help.

"Drown-proofing is even easier," Darius said. "The part people find uncomfortable is floating with your face under, just beneath the surface. Watch me!"

"Ok, with your partner—try it now," Darius continued.

"Ok, good. Let's break for lunch; try not to stuff yourselves as swimming is harder with a full stomach, as you all were taught as children. This afternoon, we are going to learn the protocols of Scuba diving. See you at 1 pm."

The group would have broken up into pairs, but Amy suggested they all go to the buffet across the street as a group, and get to know one another better.
The buffet was all-you-can-eat, which is very tempting for hungry 7th grade boys. They can eat a lot!

Amy started.

"So Perry. What has motivated you to learn scuba diving this summer?"

"I just want a new activity that challenges me," he said.

"Marie?" Amy continued.

"We don't have a lovely ocean in Montreal, just a big muddy river," she said. "I want to experience the sea, someplace warm enough to enjoy it."
She had a French-Canadian accent that was musical and made everyone realize that Canada was an open culture; French was the second language of Canada.

"Hey, my cousin is studying at Concordia University in Montreal," exclaimed Santiago. "He loves it there. People are so friendly, he says. I wanna go sometime to visit Quebec."

Marie laughed, and said: "Tres bien" in French, which was just like 'Muy bien' in Spanish. Everybody got it, and the mood of the group was a happy one.

Although Darius was an accomplished diver, he brought in a PADI-certified trainer for the next part. His name was Dennis. He was a senior at U Florida in Tallahassee.
"Never assume it works—always check *before* you dive."
Dennis was serious. He went through the routine of checking the hoses, the air supply, the belts and

how to snug them up against the tank and against your shoulders, once the full harness was on you.

Sandy was having trouble, and so were the twins.

"It's too heavy for me," they all agreed.

"It will be a bit heavy until you get in the water," Dennis said.

As if on cue, Sandy toppled over the edge into the deep end, flailing at the air.

Darius smoothly dove in and grabbed her harness. She was panicking, but everyone spoke to reassure her and she settled down.

Then everyone got in, and it turned out that Dennis was right. He even said that weight belts are often used to help a diver go down.

The lesson was over before long, and they had supervised time to play around in the pool with tank and harness.
Tomorrow they would learn how to use the mask and the fins. Then it would be open water time again.

***

The dive boat left promptly at nine a.m. Sandy and Jacklyn were not on it. Sandy couldn't handle it, Jacklyn said, and she didn't want to go without her.

Henry and Perry were totally pumped for this dive.

"You boys stay close to the boat," their parents had advised. "And don't forget to wear your lifejackets when you are not diving."

Perry was more interested in talking to Henry about marine animals, not water safety.

"I bet we see sharks!," said Henry.

"Yeah, I think we can see several kinds of sharks out here. Some—like nurse sharks, are docile; some, like hammerheads, are dangerous and I sure hope we don't encounter too many of those!"

"The instructor would never put anyone in danger, right?" Henry sounded a little unsure about that.

"OK, people, listen up." That's how Darius always started his lesson. 'Okay, people...'
He sounded like the gym teacher at Brackendale who talked exactly like that too.

"We want to start to be aware of the underwater features down there. We will be in about eighty feet of water today. Pay attention to the coral formations—don't touch them, as they are protected by law. Notice the rocks they grow on, and the kinds of corals you can see.

Then, pay attention to the fish. As you know, some—like the lionfish—have poisonous spines that stick out, so avoid them. Moral eels are nasty, bad-tempered, and lightning-fast, so give them clearance."

He paused to answer a question.

"Yeah, they look like fat snakes, and come in colors raging from puke green to black. Just stay away from the holes in the ledges where they hide. They are like dogs—if they think you are invading their territory, they'll lunge at you with their fangs.
Make sure your buddy is behind you at all times. Okay? Let's dive!"

The water was clear and about 75 degrees. They followed the dive rope down to about twenty feet, pressurized their ears by holding their noses, and then continued their descent.

The dive instructor was responsible for anchoring a guide rope to the seafloor for the students to follow both down and back up. It was psychologically reassuring to see something that connected you to the world above, *your world*.

The rope was attached either to the stern of the boat, or a bright red buoy with the familiar red stripe that indicated 'Diver Down'. Perry had seen a flag marked that way on every dive boat.

Massive fronds of kelp and sponge reached up to the light. Brilliant fish of every size darted between the rocks and coral formations, even through your legs.

Perry and Henry took turns swatting at them, but they were impossible to touch.

Talking underwater was a problem. That's why they learned a simple hand signal code. For example, 'OK' was making a circle with your thumb and forefinger and holding that posture in front of you, so others could know everything is fine with you.

Time to ascend was when you pointed to your wristwatch, and gave a thumbs-up signal. Others were common sense. Waving hands in front meant 'I have a problem'; pointing at something meant 'Look at what I am seeing'.

That is how Perry knew that the twins had been the first to see the shark.

Sharks are predators, so they don't go swimming for fun; they are on the hunt for food all day long.

It was creepy to see how they flicked their tails and moved effortlessly through the haze of particles moving in the current of the ocean around them.

Everybody just kind of stopped swimming, and froze in place, treading water seventy-five feet below the waves.

It was joined by others, perhaps curious about these visitors from topside; but soon they disappeared into the deeper gloom, looking for a victim that did not have a stream of air bubbles rising from its face.

Perry was thinking something.

If he thought about it, he would realize that Darius was probably thinking the exact same thing: where is the treasure?

Darius was off by himself, searching for something. Clues? Signs of a shipwreck?

Perry wanted to know more about this whole business of treasure hunting.

Lucky divers had recovered millions in gold and silver bullion, priceless artifacts; he understood the fire that was burning in the heart of men like Darius. It just was natural.

When they did get topside, the captain said there had been shark attacks reported in the area, some in very shallow water.

There were no fatalities, but some swimmers had serious bites on their limbs.

The enemy is hungry, thought Perry.

Chapter Three Finders, Keepers

Perry and Henry wanted to know more about the history of shipwrecks and if someone could just find one and keep the gold.

Mr. Schuyler said: 'The law seems to say 'Yes, you can.'"

The boys were now engaged in a serious conversation with their fathers, who were also boys once, and every boy likes the idea of finding treasure somewhere.

Peter knew quite a bit about the law of salvage: what the rules are when it comes to claiming an underwater shipwreck.
  "There are pros and cons," Peter Schuyler explained. "You have to think of the enormous risk as well as cost."

Robert Normal, an accountant, chimed in: "Yes, because risk usually outweighs benefits in salvage operations, as I understand it. Few wrecks contain enough cargo of value for make a fortune. There are exceptions, but they are rare."

  "Then why is our dive master, Darius Frame, so certain that he can find and get Spanish gold, Dad?"

Perry leaned over toward his father, resting his arms on his thighs.

"He must know something," said Henry.

"Why don't you boys do a little more digging around, and see what you can come up with? Where there's smoke, there's fire, right, Robert?

Perry's Dad was enjoying their vacation and was happy to agree with Peter. They had just ordered lunch, and were having a cold beer while they were waiting.

"Do you think any of the old sailors who hang around the harbor might know anything?" said Henry.

"Give it a try, Henry," said Mr. Schuyler said.

Like Perry's Dad, he wanted to encourage his boy to discover things for himself, rather than coming to him for answers. He also realized that there were many things he did not have answers for.

He pulled out his wallet and took out a fifty. Perry's Dad didn't want to look cheap, so he took out $50 as well.
"Here's some walking-around money for you boys. Go get some snack, and see what you can find out! And good luck! If I were your age, I'd be doing the same thing."

Perry and Henry headed toward the docks.

"Hey? Shouldn't we hit the library sometime? They have books on treasure-hunting in Florida, with real maps!"

"Yeah, later," said Perry. "I have a feeling we are going to meet someone today. It's just a feeling."

***

The smell of the sea, the whirling gulls screaming with eagerness to get scraps of food from the boaters, was something that inspired Perry; he wanted to dive every day.

This afternoon they would do a short trip out toward the Bahamas, if the weather was good.

An old man was sitting on a bench, tossing bread to the gulls. He looked weather-beaten, his beard was white, and the skin on his face tan and wrinkled.

"Come over here, boys. I bet you'd like to hear a pirate story."

Perry and Henry slid onto the bench.

"How do you do, sir? My friend Henry and I are down from upstate New York. And yes! We are very interested in pirates—especially where buried or lost treasure is concerned!"

"Thom Dean, at your service. I've sailed these waters for over sixty years; seen all kinds of strange and wonderful things. Retired now."

"Tell us!" said Henry.

"Yes! Tell us," said Perry.

"Out yonder, about twenty nautical miles from this very pier, is a mystery."

Henry's ice cream cone was melting onto his hand; he forgot to even eat it. Henry and Perry love mysteries more than anything.

"Some years back, I was doing some deep sea fishing out Bimini way—that's the north tip of the Bahamas island chain. The water was as clear as glass, and my sonar was pinging me that something odd was down on the bottom.

Well, the bottom was only twenty feet down, so I put on my snorkel and fins, and slipped into the water. There, on the sandy bottom, was what looked like a wall; a wall of cut stone piled one on another, running for hundreds of yards.

'Now who would build a wall underwater?' I said to myself.

Through the water, that was starting to cloud up as the tide came in, I saw another remarkable thing: stones laid end-to-end in a broad J-shape, that looked like a road, you know, those kind of stone roads the Romans built all over Europe, and which are still there?"

"You saw an ancient road with a nearby wall? Have you heard of the lost city of Atlantis? Some people think it may be somewhere off Florida," Perry was saying.

'Well, that's the thing. This wall must have been built about 12,000 years ago because that is the last time that area was on dry land. Then glacial melting in the north raised the sea level and drowned many coastal cultures. Including this one, I guess."

Perry and Henry had found their mentor in this old sailor, just sitting there on the dock--as if he had been waiting for them.

"We read that Atlantis disappeared in an awful eruption, some say it was 'overnight'."

"Yes, I know that story, too. Thing is, nobody's really explored this coast—'cept for the gold-seekers.
Oh yes. That's the other part of the story you wanted to know.

"I can tell you this, Henry, Perry, the sea does not give up its treasures easily.

More men have lost a fortune, or even their lives, hunting for Spanish and pirate booty, than you dare imagine.

But that hasn't stopped them from coming and coming—every year there's an expedition leaving this port.

Many go south to Key Largo and the Florida Keys. Lots of wrecks there.

Not so many go east, out on the Shelf, where there is another strange phenomenon— but I'll save that story for another time. I see you boys need to be going."

Perry was checking his watch frequently so that they could get to the dive club on time.

"Thank you, Mr. Dean. You have been amazing!"

"Most welcome, boys. And it's *Captain Dean*. Come by again. I'm always here."

Capt. Dean swung his hand holding a wooden match along the bench, and holding it to his pipe bowl, he drew and blew clouds of fragrant tobacco smoke into the warm air.

***

The scuba lesson had not yet started as the boys hurriedly got into their swimsuits and aboard the dive boat. Darius was on the bridge, looking at some maps, and had the door half-closed.

Amy was enthralling the crew with a story about the famous American psychic, Edgar Cayce, who predicted Atlantis would rise from the ocean floor starting in 1968.

The very word 'Atlantis' had a magnetic effect on people, and everyone huddled around her to hear what she had to say.

"He said this ancient kingdom had a magnificent culture and they had technology far beyond even what we have now. But they started to dabble in power they could not control.

They built a huge crystal that powered a device that could let them fly, or destroy enemies. Once they got greedy and used the crystal for evil purposes, it caused the island to fracture, and then the volcanic fury of the mountain destroyed their mighty city."

"Wow! That's incredible!" Not just Henry and Perry, but all of them were bouncing on the mahogany bench running below the gunwales.

"He said we would start to see proof off the coast of Florida, near a place called *Bimini.*"

Perry looked at Henry. Henry whispered: "Capt. Dean went there. That's where he saw the wall and the ancient road."

"Shhh," said Perry. "Let's keep this under our hat, for now."

"Any questions?" said Amy, seeing that Darius was now on deck and fiddling with tanks.

"Does Edgar Cayce say anything about the Bermuda Triangle?" asked Perry.

"Not directly," said Amy, "...but I have other information about that. Let's talk over dinner, if you're free."

Perry mentally noted to call his Mom and see if they could stay out later.

Darius unwrapped a new piece of equipment that most of the party had not seen before. It was a metal detector, a special model that was for underwater use.

He explained how it worked, and why this model was mainly for hunting gold. The computer could distinguish between ordinary metals that would be found on a beach, such as iron, steel, or aluminum, and precious metals—like gold.

Darius said he spent a day 'beachcombing' with this instrument, and found $1200 worth of rings, gold necklaces, and chains.

"If it's below the high tide mark, it's public property, so—finders, keepers!"

Darius had a wolfish grin on his face. You could see that treasure-hunting was his obsession. All his efforts in diving, and metal detecting, seemed directed toward the prize that seemed constantly on his mind.

"Today I will split you into teams of four; each team gets a Gold Bug detector, and will search a section of seabed I have outlined on this map. Here, everyone take a look.
    Amy and Ted will partner with Perry and Henry, the twins with Santiago and Marie. The rest of you come with me.

The unit is battery-operated and simple to use. Just do what I do; set this dial and this knob—and you're good to go!"

Ted carried the unit down to the seafloor, which was unusually clear and free of boulders at this new site.
He set the controls, and the thing started to emit a signal. Darius said the signal will speed up if you get a target.

Ted closed his fingers in the 'OK' sign, and they began to troll up and down their designated search space.

Each of them got a turn. That way, they could become familiar with how the detector worked, and could optimize its use during dive time—always too short it seemed.

Humans are not made to be underwater creatures; their life depended on an air supply, which was finite.

And if you dive deep, you must ascend very slowly in order to let the dissolved nitrogen in your bloodstream be exhaled naturally as you rose, and the pressure and darkness receded.

Perry was a little surprised when the pings got louder and closer together. The signal carried well underwater, and soon Darius was in view, coming closer.

Henry put his mask down toward the small sandy bump that seemed to be the source of the detector's interest

Darius signaled Ted and Perry to sweep the sand off whatever it was.

It was not what anybody had expected.

First of all, it was an ancient wooden box that looked a lot like a coffin. It had a lid. It was coffin-shaped to fit a human body. It was nailed shut.

But the pings came fast and thick.

Darius took his diver knife and pried at the lid. It gave bit by bit. Then it was off.

By now the whole student crew was crowded around, gawking at what had been discovered.

It was a skeleton.

It had its boots pulled off and tucked under its knees.

It wore a red bandanna and a waistcoat of the style pirates of the 1700s were known to wear. It had two gold-capped teeth that grinned at the startled divers.

In its fist was a cloth, tied in a knot.

Darius carefully pried the bony fingers of the dead man open, and removed the cloth and its contents.

It seemed heavier than expected, because Darius dropped it accidentally onto the white sand.

Something popped out at that same moment. It was a doubloon—a gold coin of great value!

Darius held it up in his outstretched hand, as if he had won the Olympics or something.

Darius had his treasure at last!

Up on deck, Darius was ecstatic. He got on the radio to someone in port and relayed the good news.

He did not say what the GPS location finder showed, however. He wrote that down in a little journal he always carried in his pack.

"Perry," said Darius when he came down from the bridge, "you are the hero today! See? I told you guys if we persist, we are gonna find hidden treasures lost for centuries.

Perry, you did well! Dinner's on me, everyone!"

Perry's Mom granted him permission, and was pleased to hear he had found lost gold on his dive today.

"Do you get some of the treasure you found?" she asked.

"Aw, Mom. I don't care about that. I just liked being part of the whole adventure. You know me."

Perry was being truthful with his mother.

But what he didn't say--maybe wasn't totally conscious of today--was that he was after a bigger treasure than a fistful of pirate gold. He was after Atlantis itself!

Chapter Four   Friends Like These...

The dive the next day carried with it all the excitement and suspense of yesterday's find. Who knew what they would find today?

They were a little further out in The Gulf Stream, and the current was stronger.

It was harder to stay in one place, so they had weight belts on that added 20 lb. to their total weight.
Underwater, that was hardly noticeable. On deck, you felt like a whale.

Perry got separated from the other three by the pull of the current.

Suddenly, out of the gloom he saw a pile of stone rubble, covered in barnacles and fronds of coral and sponge. Just out of interest, he flapped his fins with some effort, and settled in the sand right beside this curious formation.

Two questions always face underwater explorers: first, is it natural? Or, is it man-made?
Perry knew enough geology to know that rocks are part of a larger whole, they don't just appear out of nowhere.

These rocks showed evidence of having been shaped. They had symmetry. They had squared-off corners and right angles. Nature does not make right angles. This was a structure.

Perry had taken a tip from Darius, although Darius had not noticed.

Perry had a diver's knife strapped to his leg. Such knives were wide and sharp—like a Bowie knife—and had a multitude of uses when diving. Like cutting and poking into little dark places.

Perry was digging into a crevice, and scooping the residue of rock and sand out with his left hand.

He felt a shape that was about the size and thickness of his android phone, and tugged until it slid free.

He immediately noticed that it was a different kind of stone from the surrounding boulders. The color was much lighter and the surface was smooth.

And it had something so compelling about it, that Perry looked around in amazement.

It had writing; hieroglyphic symbols of some kind. A message from the past!

Perry slid it into his armpit under the wet suit, and returned to the group. Ted gave the thumbs-up signal to ascend, and they took their time, since they had been down deeper and longer than usual.

No gold today! Darius was disappointed but tried not to show it.
He spent the trip back on the bridge by himself.

That gave Perry a chance to share with Henry about what he found down there.

"We'll get it home and then take a closer look. You won't believe it, Henry."

    ***

"Why are these kind of symbols always hard to read?" said Perry.

"Yeah, they look like familiar things, like rods or birds, but make no sense at all. There is no discernible pattern that I can see."

Henry was good with identifying recurring elements in data—he was learning to program computers and create algorithms to make them do remarkable things. Henry's future career was starting to take shape.

"Let's do it like the cipher codes of World War II," said Henry. "We can infer the meaning of certain symbols, but probably they can't be read like alphabets in modern languages. Each symbol may be a separate idea or thing.

Egyptian hieroglyphics are like that. So are Native American Indian petroglyphs, carved into rock in New Mexico pueblos," Henry explained.

"This may take some time, Perry," Henry concluded.

"Too bad we don't have a Rosetta Stone, Henry," said Perry.

"Yeah, the Rosetta Stone had three languages together, and allowed a translation of the original Egyptian. That is in the British Museum in London, I believe."
Henry could be an encyclopedia of knowledge at times. Perry was glad to have him on this adventure!

***

It was hot. Florida hot. Eighty-something and the reflection off the white sand beach and water made you feel like you were in an oven.

Sunblock was essential or you would burn really bad. Marie discovered that the hard way.

So with Marie gone home, and Courtney and Santiago taking the day off, Darius made a suggestion.

Put everyone in one dive group to check out the reef—everyone except Perry.

Perry and Darius were going treasure-hunting beyond the reef using the Gold Bug detectors-- just the two of them.

Darius said Perry was his lucky charm. Perry said 'fine'.

So Henry and the others took their GoPro cameras to the reef to get a view of the diversity of flora and fauna that inhabited it, just inside the three mile limit.

Reefs are formed from coral—a protected species—and are home to a multitude of fish of every color and kind.

Beyond the reef, the character of the sea-life changed; here there were bigger and more intimidating denizens: hammerheads, mako, grey and white-tip sharks.
Barracuda that could rip an arm off with razor-sharp teeth. Sting rays with enormous wingspan that hovered and flapped through the water just a few feet above the bottom.

Perry was not someone who was afraid of everything; he was curious and tended to focus on the fun part, rather than the scary part of his newfound hobby--scuba diving.

The interesting thing was how Darius convinced him so easily to go out beyond the reef, beyond the safety of the shallows.

Perry trusted people. Sometimes that was not the best idea.

They stayed together for much of the time, working a line, sweeping the detectors back and forth, just like you do on shore, hoping to get a hit.

Perry noticed that Darius had an extra piece of equipment with him today.
It was a spear gun.
Spear guns come in two kinds: those with gas-powered spears, and those with rubber slingshot mounts.

Both are designed to impale an underwater target. Both are deadly.

Perry had not commented on it, and hadn't really noticed it until now.

Maybe it was for the sharks, it had to be for protection, he thought.

Sharks are curious. They have been known to swim up to a diver and bump them with their nose, to see what this thing is, and if it might be edible.

Perry preferred to remain inedible, so he kept a close eye on his surroundings.

As luck would have it, a rusted freighter loomed in the distance lying on its side, and Darius signaled he wanted to have a look.

They floated over the deck--all twisted metal masts and railings like something horrible had seized this hapless vessel and pulled her and her men to a watery grave.

Perry was going to poke his head down a stairwell when a white-tip shark came straight up at him out of the darkness.
He didn't really have time to react.

Perhaps the shark was startled too, because it avoided a collision with Perry and shot off toward the surface.

A close call. Perry was lucky, and he knew it. He decided to avoid stairways and closed areas of the wreck from now on.

They turned on their headlamps as the sun's light was fading and the shadows were getting longer.

The deck was buckled; the captain's bridge—the command center—was missing all the glass from the windows but the instruments were in place.

The wheel was intact; the compass however was spinning slowly, as if it couldn't determine where it was heading.

There were lifejackets floating empty, which suggested a sudden tragedy, and loss of life.

There were no bodies, no bones, no sign that humans had been on this ship.

Perry thought that was weird.

They had not seen any human remains either, on *Titanic* when it was discovered by Bob Ballard's team.
Swallowed up by the sea.

Perry made a sudden move to roll his body and turn in the tight space.

To his shock, Darius was pointing his speargun right at him.

***

"Didn't you know?" said Darius, once they were back on the dive boat. "There was a shark right behind you, and it was big. I knew I would get only *one* shot."

"No...no, I didn't even know it was there. I was inspecting the instrument panel."

"Well you can thank me for being ready to defend you," Darius said. "I really didn't have much choice. Sorry to scare you.

You have to get used to the fact that these waters can be dangerous. Not just the currents.

Anyone who dives in these waters has to be able to handle the sharks and lion fish--the moray eels...anything with teeth or poison spines. Sting rays are not hazardous unless you piss one off.

Oh, by the way. If you found something, you would tell me about it, right?"

"Sure, sure I would, Darius. But I didn't. You were with me the whole time."

Perry had goosebumps; maybe from the cool breeze, maybe from the thoughts that Darius was putting in his head. He tried to block them all out.

Then Darius turned his attention to the other divers, and inspected the shells and colored stones they had brought back.

Mementoes to put on their desks back home.

"Tell you what, Perry. Why don't you come to the beach party I'm organizing for Friday night?" Darius was saying.

"There's lots of girls--girls in bikinis with nice smiles—if you get what I mean.
And they'll be a barbecue where we roast a whole pig, Hawaiian style. This is part of Florida that you'll want to see. This is your chance. What do you say?"

Perry didn't want to say: "Let me ask my parents."

He wanted to look like a young man who could handle decisions himself.
So what if I am only eleven?

On the other hand, he always told his parents everything. This was a family without secrets. Even his sister Gabby was allowed in his room and had his passwords for Facebook and email.

It's called 'trust', Perry said to himself.

But what would they say to an eleven-year-old boy going to a more mature kind of party with probably alcohol and weed and who-knows-what and girls who wanted to play games that 7th graders were still unfamiliar with?

Perry didn't want to say 'no' to his face, so he said, "Let me think about it, okay Darius?"

"No problem, man. Just let me know by tomorrow. See you."

Then Darius was gone, walking up the gangplank and embracing a blonde who was waiting at the top. He could hear them laugh as they disappeared into the distance.

Henry startled him out of his reverie.
"Hey, Perry? How did it go out there, beyond the reef?"

"I'll tell you as we get back home for dinner."

So Perry told him every detail. Telling made it even scarier than just thinking about it did.

"You're lucky to be alive!" exclaimed Henry.

Then Perry told him about the party invitation.

"I don't think my parents will go for it," said Henry.

"You *have* to come with me, Henry," Perry said. "I can't go there by myself. Besides, I don't know anyone to talk to. Come on, Henry!"

"Okay, I'll ask."

***

Friday was also very hot. Floridians were used to dressing casual and light. They just didn't see the need for formal clothing--or very much clothing at all!

Bodies glistened in the torchlight, brown and tan, scented like the candles on the tables. This was a big party, and the amount of food and wine was stunning.

Perry and Henry were not interested in drinking, but were suddenly starving when they got to the shrimps on skewers, lamb kebabs, seafood canapés on crackers.

"This is what we came for, huh, Perry?" Henry's second favorite thing was eating.

"Totally," affirmed Perry. He had four skewers in one hand and was eating all of them at the same time.

Two girls in dayglo bikinis were giving them the once-over.

Perry looked at his food. He was hoping they would leave them alone, but no such luck.

"Hi. I'm Crystal. This is Angela. We're from Dade County but we know some people here. You live around here?"

Perry and Henry had to interrupt what was turning out to be a fine meal, which made them a little irritable.

"No, not really. Tourists. Doing some diving."

"Ohh, diving is *sexy*," said Crystal, looking coyly at the boys.

"Yeah, until you meet a shark," said Perry drily.

Crystal moved in so close, Perry could feel her body heat.

"Let's get a table together," she said.

They were drinking pina-coladas, but Henry had snagged some iced tea in cans at the bar.
"Have to keep hydrated," said Henry, since that was all he could think of to say.

Henry and Perry had not spent much time alone with girls. There were so many other things in the world to enjoy.

"What grade are you in?"

"Well, what grade are *you* in?" countered Perry. Perry was a star debater at school.

"I asked first!" said Crystal.

"Seventh grade, middle school. In Brackendale, New York. They have no beaches."

"And no sharks," said Henry.

The girls were getting slightly tipsy. Which made them silly.

"You have girlfriends?"

Crystal did most of the talking, but Angela was enjoying the exchange. Her eyes were bright with curiosity and a kind of hunger that boys at that age don't really pick up on.

"Naw, " said Henry.

"Not yet," said Perry.

"Well, do you *want* to have girlfriends?"

"We didn't come to Florida with that in mind," said Perry.

"Well we could be your girlfriends tonight. Only if you want it, of course."

Crystal was very direct, Perry was thinking.
*Is this how girls really are? I mean, when they get
to be thirteen, or whatever?*

All of a sudden, a guy that had spotted them,
invited himself over, and sat down.

"Hey, Crystal, hey, Angela. What's up?"

"Sorry, I'm Tareq," he said, shaking each boy's
hand.
"I know these girls. You'd better watch
out. They are man-eaters." He guffawed.

"Tah-reek! My man! What are you doing at this
party?" Crystal high-fived Tareq.

"Cruisin' for a bruisin'," he said.

"Where's your girlfriend?" Angela moved
closer.

"Broke up. Long time ago. Two months."

"So you are all by your lonesome, is that what
you are saying?"

Crystal seemed to be mocking him but Perry
sensed an underlying agenda, some hidden wish
perhaps.

Perry was beginning to dislike these girls.

They were annoying.
People say guys have one thing on their minds,
but these girls showed that two can play the same
game.

"Uh, we are going to go find some more food, if
you don't mind," Perry said.

The boys stood up.

"Nice meeting you," said Perry.

The girls gave them a pouty look, and Tareq
nodded and said "Later."

"Whew. Thanks, Perry. I didn't know what we
were going to do."

"Relax, my dear friend Henry. Perry always
thinks of something."

"Haha. Just like Indiana Jones!"

As it turned out, they did bump into Darius, with
his blonde, and a bunch of serious dope smokers.
"Want a toke?" said Darius, extending the joint
to Perry.

"Nope, thanks. We're just on our way to get
some roast pig. Right, Henry?"

"Right!" Henry said.

"See you, Darius. Thanks for inviting us!"

Perry meant it. He knew that Darius just wanted them to have a good time down here.

Partying was a lifestyle. Sort of goes with diving and treasure-hunting.

Depends on what you think of as 'fun', Perry mused.

The following day, Perry and Henry were on Las Olas Blvd. with their parents, having brunch, when Tareq sauntered by, then stopped and poked his head in the window.

"Hey Perry, hey Henry. Want to meet up later?"

"Sure, but no girls, okay?"

Perry's Mom shot a look at Henry's Mom.

"No worries. There's a Starbucks down two blocks. One o'clock. Cool?"

"Sure," said Perry. "See you, Tareq."

Perry's Mom looked at Perry. "A friend?"

"From the party, Mom. Didn't really have a chance to talk yesterday. He said he's doing a Master's in Ancient History. I want to know what he knows about Atlantis."

"I'm glad you are getting something out of this vacation, Perry. Gabby might come down in early August. She is thinking about it."

"Oh, great. It'll be great to see her."

The family paid the bill, and the parents all headed to the shops that this street is famous for.

Perry and Henry headed for the docks. They wanted a word with Capt. Thomas Dean.

"Captain Dean? Remember us? Perry and Henry?"

"Sure I do. I ain't senile yet! Sit down."

He tamped his pipe and lit it. "Now. Where were we?"

"You were going to tell us about something else, some mystery about the sea around here."

"Oh yes. The Bermuda Triangle. What do you know about it?"

Perry spoke first.

"I know about Flight 19, the Navy planes that flew out of Lauderdale on a routine training mission, and were never seen or heard from again."

"That was cool!" said Henry. "I don't mean 'cool' in that sense. I know those men had families. But, I mean, the mystery of how five planes just disappeared off the radar forever; that's cool."

"Never been found, those Avengers. Navy's looked."

The captain paused. "And there are many more reports of planes and ships disappearing in the Bermuda Triangle. It's a mighty big expanse of open water, with unpredictable weather, and freak storms with giant waves that can swallow a ship."

The boys faces were like full moons, full of light and wonder.

"You know anyone who...you know..." Henry looked at the Captain.

"As a matter of fact, I do. Here's what I know. I don't know everything, but this is what I heard." The old salt lit his pipe, which had a habit of going out, and began his tale.

"I had a friend who skippered a yacht for some rich folks from Virginia who came down every winter.
   When summer came, he normally put the boat in drydock so it could be serviced, you know, the hull scraped, engine dismantled and driveshaft greased. Maintenance stuff.

Well anyways, this one year, Jim Beam—we nicknamed him that because he liked the bourbon—took her out for one last excursion.

Got caught in a gale a hundred miles out. I think he didn't realize how far the Gulf Stream can pull a boat off course, but there he was—in a storm-- in the Bermuda Triangle."

The boys sat with rapt attention.

"So, old Jimmy battens down the hatches, puts the engine in LOW, and radios his position. Couldn't outrun it.
Then the radio quit, the compass went crazy, and lightning was flashing all around like he had never seen!

He did the only thing he could think of—tied himself--actually lashed himself to the wheel, and got out a bottle of Jim Beam and started guzzling it.
He said, 'At least I won't feel any pain if something happens.'
Crazy old coot! Just like me!"

Perry grinned at Henry. The boys were enjoying this.

"Then the lightning faded and an unearthly glow came from beneath the waves.

Nothing broke surface, but whatever it was, was *huge*, five, six times the size of his boat, which was a 75-foot yacht, I remind you! They say

Columbus, sailing to America through the Triangle saw a similar spooky light.

The waves settled, and the glow just faded away and—-since the liquor had pretty much knocked him out—he woke up in the morning to a calm sea, no obvious damage to the boat.

Funny thing was, he must have used half a tank of fuel getting there and getting turned around in the storm. But the fuel tank showed FULL, as if he had never left port.

His radio worked just fine and he radioed he was coming in.

When he got in and moored the boat, they asked if he was okay since they had received a radio call from his vessel indicating "Mayday! SOS!"-- which signified a real, life-threatening emergency.
When he said his radio stopped working, they shook their heads and said they had no idea, but it was good to see him back safe and sound.

How do you like that story, boys?"

"That is awesome!" Both boys spoke at the same time. "You should write all your stories down, Capt. Dean!"

He chuckled. "Oh, some day, boys, some day."

Then Perry suddenly remembered the time. "Tareq!"

"Thanks, Capt. Dean. We hope to see you here again. Do you want us to bring you something? Like a bottle of something?"

"No, thanks, Perry. I quit drinking some while ago after my wife passed. Take care now."

So they left him right there, where he always sat, smoking and studying the endless curve of sky and ocean. An old salt's life.

***

Tareq was sitting on a stool, sipping a specialty coffee that Starbuck's was famous for. He was reading *The Economist*, and looked up as they came in.

"We didn't get a chance to talk with those girls around," Tareq said lamely.

"They like you," said Perry.

"Yeah. Girls like guys who can make them laugh," Tareq said.

"Tell us about your graduate studies," said Perry.

"Well, I did my undergrad in archaeology and mythology. I wanted to continue with ancient history. I hope to get a tenured job as a prof somewhere in the state. Time will tell. Have to get my PhD first. It's not cheap, you know."

"My Science teacher has a PhD," Perry said. "From Berkeley."

"That's a good school," admitted Tareq, " but they specialize in other areas—not too many schools offer ancient history and archaeology these days."

"So why are you in it?" said Henry.

"I've always been interested in the past," Tareq said. "Someone said it is related to my past lives. I'm not persuaded about past lives and reincarnation and that stuff."

Perry looked at Henry, who gave him the 'go ahead' look.

"What do you think about the lost city, or kingdom, of Atlantis?"

"Oh *please*! Don't give me bullshit. That's all bullshit.
There's about zero evidence for it ever having existed. Just because Plato wrote about it, doesn't make it real!"

65

Perry signaled the waitress and asked for two lattes. Perry and Henry had discovered the joys of coffee recently.

"Well, don't you think there is a sufficiently widespread belief to justify the theory, and it may *only be* a theory, that Atlantis was a real civilization that had an impact on ancient cultures such as Egypt and Greece?

Henry smiled into his cup. He knew his Perry was not easily intimidated by verbal argument or opposing viewpoints.

Apparently, Tareq had a similar thought.

"You are in *what* grade? Seventh? Shit, you talk better than some grad students I know."

"Then I guess you don't have much support for The Bermuda Triangle theory, either?"

"You are right. More B.S. A few planes disappear because their flight leader didn't know the area sufficiently well, a few ships go missing in the ferocious storms that happen out there—and people think some supernatural or paranormal force has taken them to another dimension.

It's nonsense. First of all, there is *no* proof of other dimensions, or that UFOs come take people away in their saucers."

Perry looked at Henry with that look, the look that said '*Did you hear what he just said?*' Henry made a gesture with his hand, like spiraling upward, to mean 'UFO'.

Perry nodded. He was thinking: *Why did Tareq mention aliens? I didn't say anything about UFOs or aliens!*

"I have something I want to show you," Perry said. "I found it on the ocean floor quite far offshore, embedded in a strangely angular rock formation.
As a historian, you might find it of interest. I want you to tell me what *you* think; then I will tell you what *I* think."

Tareq looked at Perry. He was not mocking him now. He was studying him.

"Okay, Perry. Deal. We shall meet--same place, Monday morning, ten 'o'clock. Cool?"

"Cool." Perry shook his hand.
That was also new. Perry never did that before. It was making a statement, that he was confident, and had enough self-esteem to know what he wanted.

"I want to check something on the computer, Henry. Let's go to my room at the hotel. It's getting hot out here again. I don't think I will ever get used to the heat. Not the summer heat, anyway."

***

"I want to see if there is any hot news on Atlantis. *National Geographic* did a special on it, claiming that someone decided it was off the coast of Spain.

Everybody is using Google Earth to find all sorts of places where Atlantis could have been. Antarctica! Santorini! The Amazon jungle! It's nuts, Henry!"

"Well, that's just the point, Perry! Why is everybody looking for lost Atlantis? It must have an importance that Science does not understand. There is some mystery there. I think it makes perfect sense for us to be part of that investigation, even if there is scanty data to support that theory."

"Exactly. And we, my dear Henry, will find more data, and with others—we can prove, sooner or later, that Atlantis was a foundational civilization in Man's early history."

Perry's Mom looked in on them.

"Ready for some dinner, you two?"

"In a minute, Mom. I just have to check something. Meet you in the lobby, ok?"

"Ok, dear. Don't be too long."

"What are you searching for, Perry?" Henry was leaning in toward the monitor.

"I'm checking a story I heard on YouTube a couple of months ago, about some French archaeologists who were deep diving in the Triangle, and made an astounding discovery.
In fact, it was so astounding that the media have deliberately failed to report or advertise it."

"Which was...?" Henry said.

"These guys apparently discovered two pyramids on the ocean floor, north of the Bahamas, east of Florida—right smack in the Bermuda Triangle. Two, Henry!"

"No way!"

"Way! And do you know what else? They are made entirely of crystal. These divers could see through them.

Doesn't this remind you of what Amy said about Edgar Cayce's book on Atlantis? Crystals were a huge part of Atlantean technology.

Now here we are, in 2017, and deepwater exploration reveals a secret so important, that the news media, the government act like it never happened!"

"I know where you're going with this, Perry."

"See what I mean? I think, and I am going to go on thinking this over dinner, is that this is just more proof of lost Atlantis!

Pyramids, Henry! Not on dry land, not in the Andes or the Sahara! Here! Off the coast of America! I'm telling you, Tareq is gonna freak when I tell him."

"Can we go eat now, Perry? I'm going to die very soon if I don't eat."

"Shakespeare had Hamlet say to Horatio, his buddy: 'There are more things in heaven and earth than are dreamt of in your philosophy, Horatio!'"

"Ok, I get it, Shakespeare fan. Now do you want to carry me before I faint?"

Perry laughed, turned out the lights, and locked the hotel room behind them.

Act II Quest for Treasure

Chapter Six   Bahamas

The warm water brought many things ashore. Most of it was trash, thrown out of boats or washed out from the crowded beaches, and then carried in on the tide.

Henry and Perry were frolicking in the surf, which could be strong, if there were a storm out at sea that pushed the whitecaps and swells toward land.

On this particular day, Henry was jumping into the heavy surf, seeing if he could stay on his feet.

Something tangled his legs; he thought it was weeds. He pulled on it.

Then he screamed in pain.

Perry rushed into the surf, and someone notified the lifeguard that someone was in distress.

By the time Henry got into shore, his legs, arms, and hands were an ugly red with welts running up and down his body.

"Portuguese Man-o-war!" said the lifeguard.

He turned to his companion: "Karen? Call the office and let the superintendent know that we've got jellyfish again."

Henry was in tears.

"Okay, little buddy, we're going to get you to the hospital."

An ambulance had pulled into the parking lot, and two EMS personnel were packing a stretcher down the length of sand to where Perry and Henry were.

"Tell my Mom," said Henry.

"I will, Henry. It was a jellyfish that stung you. A particularly nasty species of jellyfish."

Perry walked with the stretcher to the parking area, and then began walking rapidly back to the hotel.

Oh no! Perry thought. *Now this! I've lost my diving buddy for maybe a week. Hope he's going to be okay.*

When the Schuylers went to see Henry, he was not in danger, but had lots of pain.
Perry's parents took this opportunity to let them be together, and decided they would take Perry to the Bahamas for a getaway.

They wanted to do some gambling at the casino in Nassau, and Perry wanted to do some diving. Robert Normal arranged for a chaperoned dive boat for Perry, and they parted for the day.

What Perry had found out on the Internet is that Bimini was not the only site with possible Atlantean ruins.

The largest island of the 700 or so islands that comprise the small nation of Bahamas was Andros --which had been found to have mysterious temples and columns in the Greek style, also just offshore in shallower waters.

If he could get some photographs, or hard evidence like his strange stone tablet, he could have something solid to show Tareq--maybe show the world!

Bahama Divers, stationed in Nassau, would pick him up and take him on a tour. They also provided all the gear: tanks, wet suits, breathing regulators, fins and masks.

On the east side of Andros was a dramatic drop, straight down for 6000 feet, in what is called 'The Tongue of the Ocean': a deep trench that was popular with really serious divers. Perry had other ideas.

Although he was not technically certified to dive in open-water alone, the dive crew could bend the rules by having him dive with a PADI-certified instructor, and only within areas deemed safe and appropriate. Perry signed the contract.

This was the big time, he thought. *I am on my own, making important decisions that could affect my health and safety, and I feel just fine with it,* he thought.

Perry explained that he was looking for sites with archaeological features, such as walls and temples.

"I know what you are looking for," said Pablo, the dive master.

"The government has set aside areas for protection and investigation. One of the best ones is Brown's Ruins, where Dr. Greg Little did some important work with the help of the National Geographic Society."

"Yeah! That's the one I heard about! Can you take me there?"

"Yes, but that one is north of Bimini. Why don't we dive Andros first. I think you will be impressed."

Perry was standing in the stern as the powerful outboard motors threw spray everywhere as they churned through the blue Caribbean, taking Perry to an adventure he would always remember.

They anchored their dive boat in a lagoon of remarkable beauty, and quiet—except for another dive boat flying American colors, which was moored across the bay, close to where the ruins were said to be.

"We're not alone," muttered Perry. He felt uneasy for some reason.

"Anyone can get a permit to dive, and in fact, diving is a major part of the tourist trade here. The government encourages it," explained Pablo.
"Let's dive, Perry!"

The blue was an exquisite shade of indigo and turquoise that could not be found in Nature anywhere but in the deep tropical sea. Perry had his camera ready.

In this lagoon, few sharks came; it was perfect for divers—especially newbies like Perry, who were still getting used to the underwater world and its denizens.

Perry signaled to Pablo that he wanted to check out some stone structures about 50 yards to the left of where they had dropped down from the boat.

There was no guide rope, no team of students, no Henry! It felt strange.

Like Bimini, there were indications of ancient culture here: walls, columns that were long enough to support a roof, and tapered gracefully at one end.

 Perry snapped picture after picture. He scraped one column with his knife, and white marble appeared under the green film of algae and crust of shells.

Marble is a soft stone and easy to carve, and has a characteristic sheen when cut.
It was marble alright, Perry noted.
Who would build marble structures in this part of the world?
Marble was a Greek invention and used to build all their famous monuments, some of which still stand.

But did the Greeks voyage across an unknown ocean full of sea monsters to found a colony in Florida?
It was doubtful. Even the Spanish after Columbus were slow to develop a colony here.

Someone was watching Perry. Someone with a black wetsuit and fins. A man.

Perry could see him duck down behind a stone beam, but his air stream of bubbles gave him away.

Was someone else on the trail of lost Atlantis? Or did they think Perry was after Spanish gold?

Most people believed gold was just lying there for the taking.

People could be desperate enough to do anything to get it—even kill. Divers had disappeared before; Perry was thinking it was time to go up.

He signaled to Pablo, and the two ascended and broke the surface.

"That was great," said Perry.

He did not mention the spy with the black wetsuit and fins they left behind.

The boat ride back to Grand Bahama Island was pure joy! Sunshine, and spray, and flying fish landing on the bow deck for Perry to inspect, then toss overboard.
He soon forgot about the shadowy figure in the depths of the lagoon.

He thought a lot about Henry. He missed his best friend. But he would share the whole thing with him tonight!

***

His parents had been enjoying the luxurious hotel on Grand Bahama, but preferred to return Stateside since The Bahamas was, in fact, a foreign country, with its own laws and customs.

Lisa Normal said she was more comfortable staying at home, in the good ol' U.S.A. No one argued with her.

Perry wanted to get to the hospital before visiting hours were over. He talked about nothing else on the fast boat trip back.

Perry was led by the nurse to the ward where Henry was.

"Perry! Wow! I'm sooo glad to see you!" Henry tried to sit up, then yelled as the painful skin was squeezed.

"Lie down, silly," Perry said. "Let me tell you what I found when I was diving today."

Perry mentioned the marble columns and the walls of carefully cut stone, set one on top of another, clearly man-made, and clearly very very old.

79

He also mentioned the spy.

"Well, who would be doing that?" said Henry.

"Your guess is as good as mine, Henry," said Perry. "Whatever they wanted, they wanted to see what I was up to."

"I wish I had been there," Henry said.

"You know what? Probably it's better you weren't. There might have been real danger, this time not from jellyfish or sharks.

I heard from Pablo, the dive boat owner, that cocaine smugglers from South America do a lot of runs to the States, using the Bahamas as refueling or hiding places. This guy could have been one of those!"

"I see what you mean. Yeah, I'm glad you got away. Show me the images you uploaded."

Soon the nurse announced it was time for Perry to leave.

"Promise me you will get well, Henry. I need you. You know it's no fun being down here without you. Do whatever the doctor says. And text me!"

Chapter Seven   Fool's Gold

One of the tools Perry was eager to get his hands on was a sidescan sonar.

This amazing device could generate an image of the seafloor as a boat or ship passed, giving any explorer a real-time picture of whatever it was down there: aircraft, sunken ship, sunken road.

Yet, for a fee, someone could access the Coast Guard archives where they kept a database of sonar scans, underwater photographs and videos, and some very detailed maps. They had topographic maps showing the contours of the seabed.

It was a huge benefit for Perry, and Henry, now out of the hospital and anxious to get on with their project.

This archival information was priceless.
    "We can't get this information anywhere," Henry said. "We could spend months in here."

    "I know. We might even have to skip lunch," Perry said with a wink.

    "No way," said Henry. "That is too great a sacrifice."

There was no indication of the mystery pyramids found in deep water in any of the files. Perry was not surprised.

But the government data did support the findings of others, and Perry himself, that an enigma exists in the water off Florida and the nearby Bahamas.

"Could it be Atlantis, Perry? Could it be real?"

"Let's assume for the moment, Henry, that we are onto something big here.

And don't forget, we still have to translate that tablet I found. It must be a key of some kind. If we find other examples of that script, that would be helpful.
But I have no idea where!"

***

Perry and Henry had one last thing to do first.

They wanted to get their official open-water certificate that allows them to dive when and where they want.

The boys huddled in Perry's room, doing the online course in PADI scuba diving knowledge, which normally takes three or four days. They did it in two.

"That last quiz was hard, Perry."

"I know. They have some tricky questions. Just like Mr. Kruschevsky, our Math teacher."

"Okay, now what?"

"Now we tell Darius we want to do the last step in the Skills component, and have him recommend us to get our certificate from PADI."

Darius promised he would do it, right after he returned from a dive with a buddy of his who is also a big-time treasure-hunter. They would be gone till Thursday.

There was little for the two friends to do, but wait.

The others in the class had departed, most wanting to give themselves more dive time before they certified for open-water. It felt lonely without them, Henry said.

***

Darius Frame was known around town as a wild card, who would drive hard to get what he wanted, and step on anyone that got in his way.

There were some who wished he would get on his boat and disappear in The Bermuda Triangle.

He was not popular, even with the dive shops who got his business. He was greedy. He overcharged students, and tried to bargain down the prices for equipment and supplies.

He was seen loading a mysterious cargo on his dive boat 'Raptor' just the other night. Sailors and merchants wondered what it was that was so important to keep secret by loading under cover of darkness.

No one knew. But people talked.

In a small marine community like this, people gossiped in bars and coffeehouses, and seemed to be quite aware of the private lives and doings of everybody. Darius Frame was no exception.

He was always up to something, was the general opinion.

So when dawn came on Tuesday, Frame and his boat were gone.

One boat passed him in the harbor, and told the folks in the all-day breakfast joint that there was no one to be seen on deck.

This was not an instructional outing, they concluded.

Maybe, maybe he was onto Spanish treasure again and he would certainly want to keep that quiet.

The sun was shining down as the two divers slung heavy sacks over the port side, taking care to hook them to the anchor line with carabiners. There were four or five of them.

Darius Frame and his companion were not bringing something of value to the surface; they were submerging it--to the sand ten fathoms below!

***

Thursday came, and the boys were ready. More than ready.

They had reviewed the online material, discussed all the lessons in the pool and in the surf.

'Preparation' is the key to everything, Perry's dad Robert liked to say. Well, they were prepared!

"Let's do it this way, fellas," said Darius. "We're gonna take you out inside the reef and we'll take you down and we can do some digging around—you never know! Might be our lucky day.

Then, once we come back, I will sign the papers that you have demonstrated the knowledge and skills of basic scuba diving, and you can apply for the certificate. Sound good?"

Sounded good to Perry and Henry!

Soon the roar and spray of the twin 250 HP marine engines took them beyond sight of land, out to the deep blue sea.

They anchored, suited up, and bailed out over the side into the warm briny waves. Only five feet down and the waves were no longer felt at all.

They went down, down, until they reached the seafloor.
Monkfish and angelfish and all kinds of colored fish swam past them, around them, without hesitation.

They were part of this environment now. They were divers.

Darius was in the lead. He was looking for something. This time he did not have the metal detector, but he didn't really need it with his experience.

Perry was thinking that Darius could smell gold, find treasure where nobody else could.

All of a sudden, Darius stopped and fanned his fins to balance himself.

He had spotted something. Was it treasure?

He motioned Perry and Henry over, and indicated they should go to that specific area.

Perry did as he was told, and landed on a rippled ridge of sand that rose slightly above the surrounded terrain.

Darius gestured in a way that meant they were to start digging with their hands.

Perry was scooping the sand off what appeared to be old sacks, like burlap or cloth. Something metallic spilled out onto the sand.

They were coins, dozens of them. They glinted in their headlamps.
They had engraved designs on them.

Henry had retrieved a cross of what looked like silver, studded with ruby and emerald stones. It was magnificent.

There were goblets of silver, candlesticks, all kinds of artifacts that seemed to show that a priceless treasure was lost to Time at this very place where they had dropped anchor.

What luck for the boys! Darius would tell the world that his two prized students found Spanish gold, and all of them would be famous!

Henry wondered where the shipwreck was.

Normally, there was a hulk of rotting timbers: the remains of the hull and decking. No sign of it.

They filled two nylon pouches that Darius had thoughtfully brought along to carry any objects of interest that might be found.

Once on deck, they spilled their trove onto a blanket.

"Wow, guys! You did it again! These are real gold and silver relics. Wait till we get ashore. You will be in all the papers!" Darius seemed happy.

Henry and Perry were too excited to stand still. They got up; they sat down. They got up again, and paced the boat from bow to stern. They took a hundred selfies.

After pulling into port, the boys noticed that the newspaper and TV reporters were already waiting.
Darius must have radioed the good news right away.

There were some other men, too.

They were wearing suits and ties, and looked a bit hot in the noonday sun. Flashes went off as Darius leaped to the dock from the stern lines.

"Mr. Frame. Can you tell us more about this find of yours?"
"Mr. Frame. Is this the find you have been waiting for?"

More flashes, a crowd forming.

"Well, it was actually discovered by these two clever students of mine-Perry and Henry. Step up to the rail, boys."

They posed proudly. Maybe their friends in Brackendale might see them on live TV! That would be awesome!

The deck was now occupied by the men in suits. At least one seemed to work for some government department or other, and one told the security officer that he was from the university History department.
Henry and Perry would have their discovery corroborated by experts!

It was very hot, and somewhat humid. Some of the suits loosened or even removed their jackets and ties.

The sun was at its zenith. Somebody brought bottled water on a hand dolly to pass out.

Perry and Henry refused to leave their treasure alone with those men, and sat in the shade of the wheelhouse.

They watched the whole process unfold.

Minutes turned into hours.

It was near three o'clock when the men rose from their squatting position, wiped their brows, and made their declaration.

"It's all fake!"

Perry nearly fainted, and Henry hung his head.

"These so-called coins are cheap imitations of brass and lead, stamped with phony Spanish seals. The same with the cross and other items. They could be bought from any toy factory in the United States."

Perry struggled to his feet.

"But sir, we found these a mile offshore, in fairly deep water. How could they be fake?"

"Well, young man, someone apparently placed these phony coins and bric-a-brac down there, and you just happened to come upon them."

"What are you saying?" Perry was indignant. His face was flushed and hot.

"This site was salted, young fella.
Now that wouldn't have been *you*, would it? Huh? Trying to get famous by claiming you found gold just by dumb luck?"

Henry now stepped up.

"That's a lie! Perry would never do such a thing! I don't know how the stuff got down there. All I know is Perry and me didn't put it there, and have no idea whatsoever about how it got there!"

The media was eating this up.
Flashes of cameras, reporters scribbling like crazy, TV people sticking a microphone in everybody's faces.

It was a disaster.

Darius, oddly enough, had disappeared and was nowhere to be found.
Later he said he had an emergency and had to leave, but missed all the action, and that he was sorry.

Now an older man with a mustache stood up, and said the following:

"I believe that these boys are innocent. Clearly they are the victims of a hoax, an elaborate prank, committed by some unscrupulous person or persons.

This is not the first time this kind of thing has happened in Florida.

Everybody wants to have a moment of glory, and fake artifacts have surfaced before. I think we can just forget this whole affair, and chalk it up to local shenanigans."

"Director, do you think charges should be or could be laid?" said a TV reporter.
The director, a government official, said 'no need.'

And that was that.

Everybody ran to the nearest bar or restaurant, the TV networks loaded their cameras and equipment into vans, and sped off.

Before too long, Perry and Henry were all but alone on the dock, feeling like a truck had hit them.

"I am *never* diving again," Henry said bitterly.

"This is not our doing, Henry," Perry said.

"Someone wants to throw us off, thwart our project.

Someone doesn't want us diving out there.

Someone with something to hide."

But it was not over just yet.

Two days later, Robert Normal got registered mail delivered to their hotel, return address Bureau of Archaeological Research in Washington, D.C.

The letter related to the diving exploits of Perry.

The letter warned that they are not permitted under federal law to hunt for treasure without having a state permit, to explore and 'recover' anything of archaeological value in United States territory, including the waters off Florida. To do so without a permit, is a felony.

"I'm a criminal, now?" exclaimed Perry.

"Well, we can do something about this, son," said Robert Normal.

"I can set up a company that can, itself, apply for this permit, and then we are legitimate—we can hunt, salvage, and keep whatever find."

"Jeez, Dad, that is pretty complicated. Is there an easier way?"

"Well, Perry, you can stop treasure-hunting. That doesn't mean you can't dive, it just means you can't bring anything up, have to leave it and probably should report to the Bureau about what it is you found."

"Why is this happening to me, Dad?"

"I don't know. Somebody has it in for you, Perry. Something that is related to your little project that you are doing with Henry. I don't see what the big deal is. So, for now, let's just play it cool. Know what I mean?"

"Okay, Dad. Let's back off on the diving for now. Until we know more."

Perry let Henry know what his Dad had said, and Henry agreed that they should lie low for a while. But that didn't mean they were giving up.

"We don't need a license to swim, Perry," Henry said. "And we don't need a license to take photographs. We have constitutional rights, and we will exercise them freely."

Perry was grinning at Henry.
"You are absolutely right, my boy. So let's go swimming, and take some pictures!"

***

In Florida, hurricane season starts anywhere from May to August, most big storms coming in

96

late August to November. These monsters spawn in West Africa, then spin across the Central Atlantic to the Caribbean, where they pick up strength and moisture and make landfall on some unlucky island or coast, sometimes Florida.

To live in Florida, old-timers say, is like living with a target painted on your roof, knowing that sooner or later, a storm will slam into your community and you will find yourself worried about just basic survival.

So the newscaster came on television, just when Robert and Lisa Normal were sitting down to a friendly game of cards with Peter and Sherry Schuyler.
The game they were playing was called 'Hearts' where penalties are given to players who are left with red cards of the heart suit at game end.
A game of winning by not losing.

The Florida State Meteorological Office has advised us that cities from Tampa on the west, to Ft. Lauderdale on the east are to be under a tropical storm alert tonight.
We repeat: there is a tropical storm warning so to give you time to prepare your community for heavy rains and damaging winds up to and including sixty mile per hour gusts.
The federal emergency management has advised all citizens to stock up on water, food, medicine,

and flashlights and blankets. Once the storm arrives, do not attempt to drive or escape on state highways. Shelter in place-- for your own safety.

We will give you updates as the storm passes through the State, provided that the electricity supply is not cut. Use your portable radio tuned to the Emergency Broadcast Network.

"Holy toledo," said Peter.

"Oh my gawd!" said Sherry.

"Where are the boys?" asked Lisa.

Robert went to peek in Perry's room; sure enough, they were playing *SuperMario* and laughing; Robert advised them a storm was on the way.

"Henry and I will duck down to the plaza and get batteries, water, and some snacks. We'll be back in a jiffy, Dad."

"What 'snacks', Perry?" Henry loved the very word 'snack'.

"*Our* kind of snacks. Anyways, our parents don't eat snacks. Mom always goes on about Dad's waistline, and how we have to be conscious eaters."

Perry went on, joking, and said, "How can you eat if you are *un*conscious, Henry? Tell me that!"

The store was getting crowded as news of the storm came in.
Emergency supplies were always the first to go. Followed by diapers, toilet paper, bandages and first aid stuff. And, of course, batteries and flashlights.

Perry and Henry loaded up on cookies ('high energy'), chips ('source of fat and salt needed in times like these'), chocolate (ditto), mineral water in one pint bottles, and frozen pizza (all round meal if power was not out).

They bought three flashlights, the kind with clunky 'D' batteries. But they worked when you needed them. Those were the ones the police use, Henry reminded Perry.

They carried all their grocery bags up to the tenth floor suites that the families had occupied for weeks now.
Peter Schuyler had managed to get the adjacent rooms to the one the Normals were in. They had a sliding door that opened into both units and made it seem like one humongous apartment.

They left the news on, while the card game progressed.

This just in from our affiliates in Tampa. A storm surge of unprecedented proportion is moving up Tampa Bay and is expected to...

Perry said to his Dad, "What does 'unprecedented' mean?"

"It means they never saw it so bad before. This is going to be a nasty one. Did you get yourself some snacks?

"Yeah, a few things."

"I'm sure Gabrielle is glad she is not here for this. Let's call in the morning and see how she is doing."

"OK Dad. Henry and I are busy. Talk to you later."

Night had fallen and the wind began to pick up.

People were hurrying home.

Boaters were tying down anything they could, arranging the bumpers along the gunwales so keep the swell from smashing their craft against the docks and pilings.

There was a mood of tension that you could almost smell. The way a wolf can smell your fear. It was eleven o'clock.

***

The waves were rising dramatically, and the noise and clash from the boats, and harbor moorings and buoys, were a warning to anyone still foolish enough to be out in the gale.

Tree branches were snapping; palm fronds were whipping to and fro as the full fury of the storm broke on Ft. Lauderdale.

Windows were heard breaking and car and house alarms sounded, adding to the chaos.

Someone's car had stalled on the corner as a flood of rain and seawater washed up and over the sea wall and poured into the roads.

This is WPLG News 10, on ABC. This is a news flash. Storm damage from Pompano Beach to Ft. Lauderdale is being reported at this hour. Viewers have reported that major portions of the Florida Turnpike and I-95 have been closed.

The Governor has declared a State of Emergency and residents are advised that they should remain in place at home. Most stores are now closed, and only hospitals are running, some on emergency power. At least 200,000 homes are now without power. Stay tuned for...

As if to confirm that, the power went off at that exact moment in the suites of the Embassy Hotel, along with the entire neighborhood.

Perry and Henry ran to the window; it was just blackness out there.

"It's time for some snacks, Perry. Don't you think? Nothing else to do!"

Henry sounded almost cheerful, like a hurricane was a good thing so long as you had snacks to munch on.

They used their cell phone light to navigate around the rooms.
Their parents had done what Robert would say is the 'sensible thing'—gone to bed.

"How long is this going to last?" Henry wondered.

"I never expected this," said Perry. "Hurricanes are something on the news, but not, like, on your street!"

Lightning shot a jagged bolt down to ground a few streets over. Someone screamed.

Someone else was downstairs near the apartment next door calling their cat.
"Here, kitty-kitty; here kitty!"

"Seriously?" said Henry to himself.

Lightning cast glaring flashes on the luxury yachts visible from their window. Thunder punctuated the angry winds and slashing rain that hammered every window in town that was still intact.

The boys somehow fell asleep through all this mayhem, and when morning came, the parents were already stirring. Someone was making coffee.

"Henry. Henry! Wake up! The power's back on. Let's go down and check out the property damage and stuff."
Perry had already brushed his teeth and was getting into his jeans.

Mr. Schuyler turned on the news.

"*Loss of life was not the big issue, Bob,*" said the broadcaster. They were already discussing the impact of the storm like it was a football game.
"*The big issue is the infrastructure. Our water supply and electrical grids are not up to par, if you ask me—.*"
Peter shut it off.

"Well, I wonder what we're going to do today," said Sherry.

The two boys were never at a loss for things to do. That was what was so great about being eleven years old.

"Mom?" Perry was asking. "Is it okay if Henry and I go down to the harbor to see what happened?"

"I don't have a problem with that," Lisa said. "Just be careful, and if you see downed wires or broken glass, just stay away from it, okay?"

"Okay," Perry replied, slurping the last of a bowl of cereal and grabbing Henry, and his jacket.

The waves were still pounded onshore, and Perry could see they were full of sand and debris. That meant that diving would be pointless for a couple of days at least. Visibility would be down to zero underwater.

Perry's cell buzzed.
    "Hello? Tareq! Hey, what's up?
    Really? Can we come? Okay, I'll tell Henry.
    When is this? Next Monday. At the college.
Cool! Yeah, see you then. Bye, Tareq!"

    "Haha, totally bitchin', Henry!
    Tareq has invited us to the Debate Club's annual presentation at his alma mater—Broward College. One of the top colleges in the country, Henry.

And he has proposed that *we* face off against *him* using the resolution that Atlantis cannot be found, even if it ever existed."

"Henry! This is our chance to reach out to other people who also believe. To provide evidence for Atlantis, evidence from right here—in Florida!"

"We'd better prepare, Perry. This is big!"

"Hey, Perry! Isn't that the jellyfish that stung me so badly?" Henry was pointing.

The beach was littered with small translucent bags with long gooey tendrils, that turned out to be man-o-wars blown in from the reef.

"It's payback time, hey Henry?" They took a long stick and perforated the gasbag.

"Yeah. One less jellyfish to sting people."

The boys turned back; they had a debate to prepare.

Chapter Nine   The Debate

Perry knew that debates are won by using two basic principles: know your stuff, and explain it logically enough for the judges to understand you. That's it.

If the boys could do this, they had a chance against an older, more knowledgeable grad student, who was fighting on his own turf, and therefore had home advantage—as they say in football.

"First of all, let's go over what we know." Perry knew that organization of your material was really, really important.

"We know that the original source was an important Greek philosopher. We also know that others have written important commentaries on Atlantis, within the last hundred years."

"Go on," Henry said.

"There is evidence worldwide that lost cities exist in certain places. Santorini was an island in Greece destroyed in a single night by what scientists call 'the single biggest explosion in ancient history'. Santorini is regarded as a possible candidate for Atlantis by modern scholars."

"Didn't you have *a time-slip* and *go back to* Santorini?"[Ψ]

"Yes, that was last autumn. Anyways, we now have further evidence that Atlantis may have reached the shores of America over ten thousand years ago.
That is what I am hoping to prove, as well, Henry. With your help, of course."

"You think that tablet with the writing that you found may be from Atlantis?"

"Yes, but we have to have more proof of that. I have to make another dive in the Bimini site."
"Right. Maybe there's more tablets!" Henry was right in tune.

"Now what we need to do is construct an argument to show that Atlantis must surely be real, and may well be off Florida in the sea somewhere."

Perry was scribbling notes in pencil, as he often did when his thoughts were coming too fast to remember.

"I don't expect Tareq to show us any mercy— he believes in what he will present at the debate,

Ψ Perry Normal & The Time Slips

just as much as *we* believe what we are going to say. It will be a classic debate confrontation; and, as you know, only one can win."
Henry was quiet for a moment.

"Hey, Perry. How about this? We let him go first, and say what he's going to say about it being just a myth, there's no proof, and so on."

"I'm listening, Henry," Perry said.

"Then once he's shot all his arrows, so to speak, we deflect them one by one but counter-arguments. Like in pro football; the winner sometimes has the better defense, rather than a powerful offence."

"That's brilliant, Henry! That gives us time to hear what he will say, and adjust our statements to cast reasonable doubt on his.

That's what they do in criminal law: create the possibility that there is inaccuracy or truth in the opponent's case."

Perry was up, dressed, and had his pack ready.
"What time do we have to be there?"

Henry checked his watch. "In two hours."

"Okay, let's have a quick lunch, and get a taxi. It's not far, but too far to walk, and the buses are unreliable because the storm caused quite a bit of damage."

The taxi dropped them off at the Omni Auditorium on the North Campus of Broward College. Once inside, ushers directed them to the backstage area where they could do final preparation. They even had a private dressing room, like Hollywood stars.

Henry's nerves were making him jumpy.

"I'm glad I'm not the one on stage. I would probably faint or wet my pants standing up there in front of all those people.
Do you know, Perry, that the Number 1 fear of Americans is Public Speaking? It's true! Research has shown that.
You know what the Number 1 fear of the British public is? Spiders! Quite a difference. I like spiders."

Henry was babbling, as he always does when he is super excited or very nervous.

Suddenly—applause. A voice was speaking into the P.A. system.

"Good afternoon, ladies and gentlemen, students and alumni. We are pleased to present our 22nd Annual Academic Debate for you today.

*We have an unusual resolution on the table
today: 'Is there evidence that the lost city of Atlantis
really existed?'*

*We know you're going to like this one. We
welcome back our very own alumnus, Tareq
Williamson.*
*And the challenger, from Brackendale Middle
School in Brackendale, New York: Perry Normal."*

Thunderous applause greeted the debaters as
they took their place at their respective podiums.
There were more people here than Perry or
Henry had imagined.

Perry adjusted the mic on his collar, and the
one on the gooseneck from the podium. The
announcer tossed a coin to see who would go first.

For a moment, Henry was dismayed—if Perry
had to start, they hadn't prepared properly. He
crossed his fingers and closed his eyes.

"The opening goes to Tareq Williamson."

The game was on!

"Thank you, Mr. Speaker. Let me begin by
addressing the fundamental flaw in the question
of whether there is, or *was*, such a place as
Atlantis."

Tareq looked very tall and handsome up there, dressed in a linen suit, every hair in place, his beard trimmed, his voice strong and clearly heard at the back of the spacious auditorium.

"In my view, the alleged writings of a Greek philosopher who lived over two thousand years ago is hardly what I would call 'proof'.

Moreover, the transcripts of Mr. Edgar Cayce and his conversations while he was under trance and later claimed they were true messages from beyond our world—well, I can hardly accept those as proof either."

The audience was deathly quiet. Their former debate champion at Broward was as sharp as ever, as direct as a sword thrust.

"In addition, since the Greeks and the Egyptians were the origin for this myth of Atlantis, it stands to reason that the evidence should be found in or near the Mediterranean Sea—but no conclusive evidence has been found.

Plato claimed Atlantis existed 'beyond the pillars of Hercules'; well, there have been arguments about what he was referring to.

Was it the Straits of Gibraltar near Spain? Was it somewhere in the Greek Islands? Was it near Sicily? Malta? North Africa?

Did this geographic landmark even exist at all, except in Plato's half-baked story that had originated in Egypt he said, from some guy named Solon?"

Perry was trying not to look up; the lights were blinding, and the audience was looking right at him, perhaps wondering what he could answer to Tareq's withering opening arguments.
    Perry was wondering himself.

"Mr. Normal? Do you wish to reply to Mr. Williamson?"

Perry cleared his throat, took a swig from his water bottle and said: "Yes, Mr. Speaker, I do."

"One of the reasons Plato is studied in American universities and colleges today," Perry began, " is precisely because of the wisdom and rhetorical skill he possessed."

Perry was going to pull out all the stops. Use every fancy word in his vocabulary. He was going to be like Lincoln at Gettysburg!

"Plato is not some idle commentator. He was the student of Socrates—the Father of Wisdom, *Sophia* in Greek.

Secondly, the story has archaeological roots in Mesoamerican culture, in Incan and Mayan culture. Atlantis is intrinsic to the folklore of Europe and America.

It is more than a simple bedtime story. It is an archetypal civilization that may well have been the basis for all civilizations to follow: Mesopotamia, Babylon, Egypt of the Pharaohs, Greece, Rome. That would explain the worldwide fascination for the legend.

And may I remind you, 'legend' has a basis in fact; 'myths' do not.

Atlantis, in my view, was a real place, with a real history, that so deeply impressed ancient scholars and writers, that the story is still very much alive today."

The audience roared its approval. It took some minutes for the clapping and whistling to die down enough for the speaker to say:

"Rebuttal, Mr. Williamson?"

"Mr. Speaker, I would like to ask my worthy opponent to present other support or evidence for Atlantis."

"Mr. Normal?"

Perry surprised them all by having the screen come down, and displaying a PowerPoint with all his photos from Bimini, Andros, the reef dives—

even one showing his tablet-- in case someone had some clue about what it might mean.

He also included the article that showed the Bimini Road, and how the divers found it and tested it, analyzed it, and had photos and sidescan sonar imaging to show that something *real and physical* exists in the deep water off Florida.

What started as whispering, became a murmur-- then became an outright discussion in the audience, as Perry took them through his visual argument that proof was out there, in the Atlantic.

"This is why this ocean is called 'Atlantic', ladies and gentlemen.
It is, I submit, the resting place of a mighty kingdom that stretched thousands of miles across, and whose remains are visible off our shores."

Since the speaker could not suppress the excitement of the crowd, he called for a recess, for lunch.

"You got them, Perry. You nailed it!" said Henry.

"Not so fast, Henry. Tareq will come back ferociously, I just feel it. Let's grab a sandwich and regroup. We only have an hour."

The bells in the clock tower outside struck 'two'. It was time.

Tareq adjusted his tie to loosen it; it was warm inside, and those lights could burn toast with their heat.

"Mr. Speaker, ladies and gentlemen, worthy opponent. We have all been impressed by the photographic evidence, the archaeological exploration done in the ocean, the Google Earth images that are very suggestive of a landmass off our shores.

But, really...is that sufficient? To say a lost civilization is right under our noses, and we didn't realize it?"

Tareq was hitting his stride.

"Where, may I ask, is the interest in the diving community? In the archaeology community? The historical societies that are tied to some of the most scholarly resources in the world?"

He went on.

"Why hasn't the Coast Guard, or the Navy reported any findings about pyramids or lost temples and ruins?

I will *tell you* why—there *aren't any*!!"

The crowd grumbled, someone booed. He was getting to them.

"Surely our federal and state governments, who have legislation in place to protect our underwater heritage, would have flagged these sites, if they exist, as important, and protected them from indiscriminate diving and treasure-hunting?"

"The only *Atlantis* in this part of the world is a luxury resort in the Bahamas!"

People clapped and laughed, nodding their heads, finding Tareq's comment amusing.

Perry was not amused, however.
What do I say now? They believe everything he says. I have one last thing to say—either this works, or I'm done.

Tareq sat down, with a smug look on his face. He smiled at them, like he was a star. A pretty girl in the audience called and waved: "You rock, Tareek!"

The speaker looked at Perry. He stood up to the podium. He dropped his voice to almost a whisper.

"My worthy opponent might feel differently if I showed him *this*!"

The house lights were dimmed, and an underwater image was projected onto the big screen; it showed what looked like two huge pyramids sitting at the bottom of the sea.

They did not look like the ones in Egypt, they were not made of stone blocks. They each appeared to be one large piece—of pure crystal!

"Ladies and gentlemen, these crystal pyramids were discovered several miles off our east coast in Florida, at a depth of close to a thousand feet.
    The French team of scientists who discovered them last year located them using sonar and submersible ROV imaging.
        It is too deep for scuba diving, but the photographs have been verified, and even reported to the United States Navy.

The law says that artifacts and wrecks in international waters belong to the finder—in this case, the French government.

I'm not making this up—these pyramids are real, and huge—hundreds of feet on a side.

Now I ask you? If the United States government does not know about them, and would not have been likely to construct them at the bottom of the

Atlantic, then who built them? And for what purpose?"

Perry explained the hypothesis that Atlantis used advanced crystal technology to create a power source for their entire island of Poseidia, named for the God of the Sea."

Perry turned to the screen again, and the audience followed him, as if hypnotized.

"Here is another recent discovery in underwater archaeology."

A vast complex of temples and buildings, including small pyramids, swam out of the sparkling, aquamarine depths, in this stunning photographic display that Perry had prepared.

"This is Cuba. Northwest off Havana, at a considerable depth, lies this lost city. You can see the architecture shows skilled engineering and design.
Now who built this? Not the Spanish. This site is estimated to be at least nine thousand years old.

I am going to suggest to you, ladies and gentlemen, that even if this is not lost Atlantis, is is *tangible proof* that there are ancient cultures we have *not* discovered, have foolishly ignored or denied the evidence for, and that we cannot afford to overlook the potential historical significance of such sites. Thank you."

Perry sat down and the people got up; it was a standing ovation. Perry smiled shyly. Henry was offstage jumping up and down, shouting: "Way to go, Perry!"

Tareq hung his head, then rubbed it, then stood up slowly.

"I see that my worthy opponent has made an impressive case here. I cannot deny that these astonishing discoveries may well point to the possibility of lost Atlantis. I have not had a chance to keep up on my reading, and I see I have work to do.
I would like to thank the College for hosting us, thank the judges and the audience for being here today. I will await the decision of the judges."
He didn't have to wait long.

Each of the three judges raised a flag of a certain color: 'white' meant that Tareq had won the debate, 'blue' meant that Perry had.

Three blue flags were held aloft, as the cameras flashed and the audience cheered.

"Stand up, Perry," shouted Henry. "Go shake his hand, or something."

Perry strode out into the limelight and accepted the trophy the speaker handed to him.

He was too shy to say any words at all, so he bowed awkwardly, shook Tareq's hand vigorously, and returned to the wings where Henry was waiting.

It was over, and once again, Perry had shown his ability to convince people—not by emotion, but by facts.
He was a scientist, albeit a junior scientist. Science can prove anything. That was Perry!

Chapter Ten   Too Close For Comfort

Gabrielle, Perry's older sister, had flown down to join her family, after a grueling summer school spent in the Science lab. She was only too happy to shed her heavier clothing for a tank top and shorts.

"It is sooo nice to get some sun on my body," she cooed. "I want to try scuba diving, too. Can I arrange a lesson with your dive master Darius?"

Perry was not happy about it.

He had definite suspicions about Darius. Every time Perry seemed to be getting close to finding something underwater, something happened.

Although he wondered how it was that Darius led him and Henry right to the fake treasure, he couldn't prove anything.

He wondered if Darius had been the spy at the Andros Island dive. Things just didn't add up.

In any case, he owed it to Gabby to show her around the harbor, and maybe let her try her hand at scuba diving with a trained professional, rather than with her little brother.

"I'll text him. See if he's available."

Gabrielle was a member of her high school's swim team, so the swimming part was no problem. She was entirely unacquainted with scuba diving gear, however.

"Show me how to get the regulator working, Darius."

Darius Frame was happy to have a new student, judging by his very friendly manner. At $80 per hour, including preparation and on board training, he was raking it in. He charged per person, of course, so Gabby, Perry, and two other trainees made it quite worthwhile to go out to the reef today.

Besides, the surf was quiet, the ocean peaceful and flat as glass.

"Perry? You're going to buddy up with Mark and Lisa here, and I'm going to show Gabby the reef, and how to pass in and out without harming the coral."

Every time you go down, it's a new experience, it's like you've never been in this underwater

wonderland before. This was all new for
Gabrielle.

What most impresses is the colors; some are
subtle like the pinks and cream of the coral, some
are brilliant and vibrant—like the parrotfish or
the zebrafish.

Perry motioned to the others to sit on the sand
and practice the signals. They had to learn to
compensate for the Gulf Stream current that
flowed day and night, carrying warm Caribbean
water north, along the American coastline, then
out, crossing the entire Atlantic Ocean to Britain.
That is the reason Britain is much warmer than its
northern neighbors in Europe.

Darius waved at Gabby, pointed to a gap in the
coral and pointed—toward the open sea.

If Gabby was concerned, she didn't show it; she
slipped through the gap in the stone and coral like
she was a tropical fish herself!

Outside the reef, the current was stronger, and the
water deeper. Gabby wasn't sure how much time
was left on her tank. She had forgotten to ask
how long a tank of air would last.

But she *knew* the dive master knew, and that was
fine.
But where was he?

Gabby looked around and found herself alone.

Without a guide, without any navigational aids like a compass, it was very, very easy to be completely lost out there.

And right now, Gabby was lost--and starting to panic.

Meanwhile, Perry was enjoying helping these two holidayers from New York City have the trip of a lifetime, stroking the big sea turtles, flipping and playing tag with each other in the warm water surrounding them. GoPro cameras built to be waterproof, captured the moment. It was perfect.

Except for one thing: where were Gabby and Darius? They should be back by now.

He signaled to the couple to go topside in about five minutes, following the dive rope back up the way they came.
He was not worried about *them*. He was worried about his *sister*.

He tried to remember which direction Darius had taken.
On instinct, he kicked his legs hard to get the fins to propel him to the left, where the reef had less sharp coral and more weedy rocks.

He saw the gap. *Is this where they went? I can't tell.*
Perry decided to shoot through and have a look, since neither of them seemed to be inside the reef.

He carefully swam along the reef wall, feeling the tide pulling him out, and making him cling to the reef in places.
Where are you, Gabby? Are you out here?

He looked for air bubbles, the best sign that there are divers down; but—nothing.

Perry began to realize that he was alone now, beyond the safe zone inside the reef. Out here, with the waves, the vast waters stretching out forever, and of course—the sharks.

That made him even more anxious for his sister.

He didn't trust Darius. Not anymore. Too many coincidences.
 Darius was greedy and selfish. He didn't give a hoot about other people. Just the money and his fantasy of finding more treasure troves beneath the sea.
He was not above using his students to help him find it. Perry saw that now.

Was Darius using his sister to help him scout out possible treasure sites? He didn't know.
He had not even thought of it—until now.

Where were they? He had looped back on the reef and felt his way along the wall, a little deeper this time.

Below him he saw a shark circling something. Did it smell blood? Did it spy a target for its next meal?

Perry circled in on what the shark was interested in.

It was Gabby!

She was huddled on the sea bottom, breathing very slowly as the bubbles were separated by ten, fifteen seconds.

He took his knife and clanged his tank; that got the shark's attention--who veered off and disappeared into the darkness.

It also got Gabby's attention, who jumped up and waved frantically at Perry.

Once he got to her, he gave the signal to surface, and he put his arm around her waist, leading her closer to the reef face so they could have handholds to assist their ascent.

But she was signalling that she was out of air! *Now what?*

Luckily Perry had practiced the maneuver to share air-- if your buddy runs out.

It seemed a long way to the top, as Perry held his breath and passed the mouthpiece on his regulator to his sister.

She would take a breath; *he* would take a breath. She would take another breath, then *he* would inhale, while she let a stream of bubbles rise, rise up to the sunlight and air above.

When their faces broke the surface, Gabby gasped, breathing hard and trying to talk at the same time.

"Oh my gosh, Perry. I didn't know... I wasn't sure if...". She kept panting, trying to get more oxygen into her system.

"Okay, Gabs. You're okay now, I've got you. Let's figure out how to get back to the dive boat, *if* it is still waiting for us."

Perry was angry. Perry was disappointed and shocked that his own sister was left to die by a man he used to trust.
Perry was going to do something about this.

When Perry and Gabby finally hauled themselves up the ladder to the deck of the boat, they were surprised to see all three of them drinking cold beer and laughing like nothing at all was wrong.

"What's so funny?"

Perry ripped off his mask and fins, slipped out of his harness and was now standing in front of the deck chairs, in front of Darius.

"My sister almost died out there, and you guys are here enjoying a good time."

"Oh, I thought she was okay, and wanted some dive time by herself."
Darius was trying to excuse himself.

Perry lost it.
"That's fucking bullshit, Darius! You know damn well she expected you to buddy her out there. You just left her!"

"Look, I'm sorry. This is a misunderstanding. I came in, expecting her to be back at the boat. I wasn't worried. I know she could handle herself. It was an accident, that's all."

Darius put down his drink, and retreated to the bridge to start the engines.

The New Yorkers were embarrassed and heading down below to get changed.

Perry sat, wrapped Gabby in a beach towel, and held her close until they got into port. When they went ashore, they didn't even so much as glance at Darius Frame.

Act III   The Real Treasure

Chapter Eleven   A Three Hour Tour

"Henry, we are going out on a boat. You wanna come?"

"Sure. Can we rent some dive gear before we go?"

"Absolutely. My Dad has a chartered boat waiting for us. There is a dive shop right there at the pier. Tell your folks. We should be gone for three hours, or thereabouts."

"Cool. What time?"

"Be here in an hour. Bring your GoPro and your dive watch. Bye."

"I couldn't make up my mind," Mr. Normal said. "Whether I hire a fishing boat with crew, or a pleasure boat, just for us. So I flipped a coin."

"You did not!" said Mrs. Normal. "You wanted this to be our own private party."

"Guilty," said Mr. Normal. "Let's go down to the Bahia Mar Yachting Center and see what they've got lined up for us."

The Barrier Island gives a natural breakwater and protective stretch of beach to the harbor at Ft. Lauderdale. The lovely Las Olas Beach covers much of it; the rest is moorage for commercial rentals like the one Robert Normal was interested in.

The shop manager was going over the features of the boat: a 43-foot Chris Craft, a classic, with teak rails and decks, sleek hull design, modern cockpit instead of a bulky bridge for the controls. Perry saw his Dad take out his credit card.

"Come on, Henry. Let's run across to the dive shop and get some tanks and regulators. We'll be leaving soon. They will deliver it right to our boat there, floating at anchor. Did you bring money?"

Soon all was ready, and the Normal family, accompanied by Henry Gerrit Schuyler, stepped down the gangplank to the pier, and out to where the Chris Craft was bobbing in a gentle swell.

The manager was explaining where certain things were, such as the anchor and windlass, the Coast Guard emergency beacon if they ran into trouble, the fire extinguisher, the engine controls.

Mrs. Normal was already pulling up a deck chair near the bow, and slathering sunblock on her shoulders and arms. She had worn her bathing

suit under a serape, and had leather sandals.
Gabby wore pink shorts and a yellow tank top,
and stowed her towels and bathing suit below in
the galley.

Perry and Henry carried the cooler with the
sandwiches and drinks, and hoisted it over the
rail and onto the deck in the shade of the cockpit.
They had food for days, even though they
wouldn't need it.

The manager wished them good luck, and pointed
them out to the narrow exit to open water.

"Did you bring my purse," Gabby asked. "And
my camera?"

"Got it," Perry said. "You want your
sunglasses?"
The water was unbearably bright in the late
summer morning.

Mr. Normal started the engine with a roar--that
made Henry smile and high-five Perry.
This was going to be amazing, both boys agreed.

They secured the tanks and dive gear on the stern
deck under a tarp, to keep them from rolling
around or getting damaged.

Mr. Normal—who now insisted on being called
'Captain'—opened the thermos of coffee, poured a

cup, blew on it, and sipped, making an 'ahh!' sound, as he started cranking the wheel to his left as the entrance opened up before them.

In fifty yards they were on the open sea, the mighty Atlantic, nothing but wind and waves all the way to Portugal and Spain.

Of course, they were only going as far as the second outer reef, or maybe try their hand at fishing for mahi-mahi, or for kingfish.

Robert Normal had a dream of one day coming to this coast and going fishing for sailfish—one of the most prized sport fishes, and one of the hardest to catch.

Today, he was living his dream. He looked like the happiest guy on earth.

"Perry! Henry! Break out the fishing rods. Set lures on the line and mount the whole business in the davits set in the rails.
Yeah! Those metal holes. They lock in the rods with that pin there, so you don't have to hold the rod if you have hooked a big one! Isn't that great?"

Perry and Henry did as they were instructed. They decided not to use live bait, which was messy and stinky, but artificial lures that fishermen everywhere use to attract fish to the hook.

Fish were not stupid. The lure had to look realistic, like a tasty piece of squid, or a smaller fish that larger ones hunted for food.

Some lures add a flashing piece of metal called a spoon, which resembles a fish moving in the bright sun, and can easily induce a fish to strike.

But fishing was not what Perry had come for. He was keeping one eye on the reef and distant small cays where the water was shallow and clear.

Sometimes you get a feeling that today will bring you something exciting; Perry had that feeling. He said so to Henry. Henry nodded and smiled.

The powerful boat cut through the water, its bow slightly raised with the thrust of the engines, spray hurled backward into a roiling wake. They had gone quite a distance and the land looked much further off.

These were the very waters the great explorers and colonists had sailed to the new land they called 'America'.
Columbus thought he had found India, and named the natives 'Indians'—a name which came to be applied to all native peoples in Central and North America.

"Look, boys! Look at that fish leaping! Is that a sailfish?"

Mr. Normal had geared the boat down to trawling speed, about four or five miles an hour. Fish won't bite if you go too fast, he explained to the boys.

Perry and Henry both grabbed the rod handles and started reeling the line in.

But they were disappointed; the line went slack. No fish on the other end.

Gabby and her mother were setting out lunch on the open deck up front.

They scrounged a table and tablecloth from the galley below, and had made a nice spread for the family. She had brought tunafish, egg salad, and smoked turkey on kaiser buns. She had dill pickles. She had a beet salad with walnuts.

There was even a pecan pie, a Southern specialty. Henry was not fond of tunafish but he was very interested in the pie.

"Wouldn't it be funny if we caught a tuna today?" said Perry.

Everyone giggled.

"Great," said Henry ironically. "Then we can make *more* tuna sandwiches."

No sooner than those words had escaped Henry's lips, the line on rod #2 zinged as something seized the hook and began to pull on the line, as the fish tried to escape its predicament.

"Just keep your finger on the reel and tighten the knob just a hair," said Mr. Normal.

"Lift up on the rod to put pressure on the fish. Let it down, and then lift again. Fish will fight you, rather than just give up and be pulled aboard. That is precisely why it is such a popular sport!"

Perry was getting tired, and let Henry do the pulling and releasing for awhile.

Suddenly, a big splash right off the port rail!

What is it? Perry wondered.

"It's a tuna!" shouted Mr. Normal. "A bluefin! It's huge!"

He took over the rod and slowly worked the fish toward the port side of the boat.

Perry took the net and struggled to slip it under the big fish.

135

Once they got it aboard, it flopped and then settled.

"Ewww, it's slimy," Gabby said, stroking the dying fish, as if to comfort it.

"You don't expect me to cook that do you, Robert?" Mrs. Normal looked with wide eyes at the four-foot monster at her feet.

"Haha, let's get it to the dock and have someone gut it, and deliver to the seafood restaurant we like. I'm sure Chef Robbie will know what to do with it. Barbecued would be nice!"

Perry and Henry twisted the hook out and slipped the fish into a galvanized metal tub like a bathtub full of ice, and weighted down the lid.

"That should keep until we get back," Mr. Normal said, beaming with pride.

"This might be a record," Henry said. "This might be one of the biggest fish ever caught off Ft. Lauderdale!"

"Yeah," said Perry. "And we will get our picture in the papers!"

As it turned out, they *did* get their picture in the papers, but not for this.

For something else altogether.

***

The sky was clouding over. The wind had picked up, and sending salty spray into their faces.

"We should go back, Robert," Mrs. Normal said.
"I guess so. Let me check the marine radio and see if I can get a weather update."

'The ridge of high pressure makes it a perfect day to be on the water. Winds will be light, out of the southwest, temperature in the high '70s. No precipitation or storms on the radar for the next 48 hours.'

"That doesn't make sense, then, because the weather right here is brewing up a storm. Are we a long way from land? I can't tell. The instruments are acting up. The compass is spinning like it doesn't know which way North is!"

Robert Normal was, for the moment-- lost. Without a compass, with the GPS giving nonsense readouts, they were alone on the wild Atlantic.

Right on the edge of the Bermuda Triangle. That is what Perry suddenly realized.

The wind was worsening. The waves were getting rougher and choppy, with whitecaps breaking and reforming immediately. Their boat was being pushed around and soon Captain Normal could not control it at all.

"Get down below!" he shouted.
They leaned on the galley door that led topside to get it to close.

"I'm getting seasick," said Gabby.
"Me too," said Henry.

The boat was rocking so hard they had to lie down on the bunks and hold on to whatever they could grab.
There was a crash, and their lovely tuna and its tub went over the side, as they would discover later.
Alone at sea, in a gale, their tiny boat was tossed.

It might have been an hour, it might have been four—nobody could tell. But the tossing stopped, and the boat was still.

Mr. Normal and the two boys climbed up the stair to the stern deck.

The boat was beached on a sand bar on a small island.

The palm trees waved gracefully in the light breeze, and the sun was still high in the western sky.

"The GPS is working again!"

"Where are we, Robert?"
Mrs. Normal was holding Gabby, who was wrapped in a shawl, and looking pale and worn out. She had lost the contents of her stomach during the storm.

"Ah, we are somewhat off course. This is close to the Bahamas. One of the little island cays, not too far from Bimini Island."

Bimini? Perry's ears perked up. *I can dive here!*

"Henry! Get into your harness. We're going diving!"

Mr. Normal was trying to raise the Coast Guard on the radio. His cell phone was not operational as there were no cell towers nearby to relay the signal.

"Come in Lauderdale. Come in United States Coast Guard. Mayday."

Only the sound of static crackled in the air.

But Perry and Henry were already under, beyond the sounds of the surface world. The water was transparent and warm.

In fact, the only way they knew for sure they were underwater was the brilliantly-colored fishes that came right up to their masks, as if to say: "Who are *you?*"

Perry showed thumbs-down—the signal to go deeper. A trail of bubbles was all that could be seen as they disappeared behind a ledge of rock and coral.

There were stones lying all jumbled up, but they had sharp edges, they were squared off; which means humans had shaped them with tools. Humans from long ago.

Perry was optimistic. It was a place just like this where he found the tablet with the writing. *There must be more,* he told himself. *There must be!*

Henry was waving frantically; he had found something.

He was cleaning the sand and silt off a small smooth flat stone.

Perry was nodding his head, and pretending to clap his hands.

Henry had found another tablet. With the same strange glyphs, the mysterious code or language.

Then he found another.

Perry tucked them into his waistband and flapped his fins to take him over the whole area.

Henry was snapping pictures with his GoPro. Including a selfie. Later, when he examined the selfie, he caught sight of the nasty green moral eel slithering out from the ledge behind him.

There was a wreck or something just ahead of Perry. He signaled Henry.

But it wasn't a wrecked vessel—it was a structure that looked suspiciously like those Greek temples in the magazines--the ancient marble columns, the capstones on the columns carved in swirls; this was a temple!

A temple means religious rituals, means an advanced civilization was once here-- in this sandy seabed-- and was swallowed by the sea ages and ages ago.

Their air supply was dwindling, so they took a few last camera shots and made their way to the surface, close to the beach.

"Dad! Dad!" Perry was trying to get his father's attention.
Mr. Normal was speaking to someone on the radio but the transmission was garbled and cut out frequently.

"Mom! Mom!" Perry kneeled on the sand by his sister and his mother.

"You won't believe what we saw!"

"Yeah," said Henry. "A lost temple or city, or something. It was just incredible!"

They both were talking at once.

"Okay, everybody. The Coast Guard is on its way. I radioed the GPS coordinates. We are going to be rescued!"

Mr. Normal was clearly relieved. He didn't want to be stranded like those characters on *Gilligan's Island*, his favorite TV show from the 1960s.

"What about the boat, Robert?"

"We'll let the rental manager know; I'm sure they can tow it, or get the engine restarted. I certainly can't.

Don't worry, honey. I'm sure this kind of thing happens all the time out here. They must be used to it."

Perry was checking out the two tablets with Henry.

"Look, Henry! Same repeating characters as on the tablet in my room at the hotel."

"I have an idea. I can develop an algorithm, a search algorithm--that will speed up the process of decoding these characters. If I only knew where to start."

The thunder of the Coast Guard cutter's engine interrupted their discussion.

"That was fast! Thank you so much!" Robert Normal was saying to the officer who came ashore from a rubber dinghy.

"Right. Everyone in good health? No injured?"

"No sir," said Lisa Normal. "Thank God!"

"Alright, let's get you out of here."

The group settled into the bottom of the dinghy, which was a sturdy Navy version of the ones commercial vessels carry as lifeboats. The officer pulled the cord and the outboard sputtered to life.

They reached the cutter and climbed the last little way up the side on a rope ladder.
This was like a movie, the boys were thinking.

Gabby wanted her bed.

Once back in port, Mr. Normal filled in the forms and cleared everything with the boat rental.
"See? I told you! They know how to handle this kind of thing."

"Let's get a cab back to the hotel," Mrs. Normal said.

The three children walked hand in hand to the minivan, and piled in.

"Henry? Let me tell your mother we are back. She must be worried. We are two and a half hours later than we said we would be."

'Hi, Sherry. Yeah. We're back. Everyone's fine. God, I need a drink. Let me change and I'll be over shortly. Bye.'

Henry was explaining to Perry how an algorithm works, in Perry's room.

Gabrielle was already asleep. Perry was silently laughing to Henry when he could hear her snoring.

"Send me the pictures you have."
It was Professor Wegener at Cornell.

Technically, he was an expert in astronomy and astrophysics. But he had a fascination for ciphers and codes, and ancient languages were of particular interest to this middle-aged scientist.

He had been part of Perry's world since Perry won the Science Contest at school last year, for his model of a wormhole that might explain how time travel would work.

He emailed them the next day.

"I don't recognize these; no, I don't think I have ever seen anything like these hieroglyphs, Perry. Where did you get them?"

Perry was sure that he could tell the Professor, in confidence, about the tablets. He decided not to go too far, and bring in the temple they had just found. *Just do this a bit at a time,* Perry was thinking.

"What color did you say the tablets were? Not black? Well, then they are terrestrial in origin. Have to rule out the meteorite hypothesis right away."

"You mean they could have come from outer space? From an alien civilization?"

"Well, not in so many words. Science has not proven there are civilizations in the Milky Way galaxy, near enough to us to try to communicate."

"I never thought of that! I was really focused on, well, Atlantis."

"As I always say to you, Perry, find the proof. Science is about *proof*.
Give me a few days to play with this code, and I'll get back to you. Sound good?"

"Thank you, Professor Wegener. I really need your help."

"I'll be in touch. Goodbye, Perry."

***

When Professor Wegener did get back to Perry and Henry, he had both good, and bad, news. He called them.

"Here's the good news. It is a human language, and has many characteristics of languages spoken all over the world. In some ways it resembles Sumerian and Babylonian cuneiform--and in some ways-- the scripts of the old Inca in South America."

"What's the bad news, Professor?"

"The bad news is I haven't got a clue what it says."

Perry could not hide the disappointment in his voice.

"I see. Well, that is useful information, sir. Thank you for taking the time to inspect the tablets. We'll let you know if we make any breakthrough at our end."

"Sorry I couldn't be more help, Perry."

"Not at all, Professor. It's a brand new discovery, and nobody alive has ever decoded or translated it. This is unknown territory for archaeology. Goodbye for now, sir."

Perry hung up the phone, looked at Henry, and shrugged.

"What now, Sir Henry? The King is of no help to us—what say you?"

Henry smiled and said: "Computer science will vanquish the enemy of Ignorance!"

And so, as always, the boys—just the two of them—marched forward on the voyage of discovery. Here was a real puzzle, and a chance to learn something about human history that had never been revealed before.

***

"Let's assume this character here—the star—means something important, symbolizes a revelation or discovery or something."
Henry, who was better at Math than Perry because he had that kind of mathematical mind, was laying the groundwork.

"And this character, which resembles a human standing, with legs a little apart, represents...well...people, the human race. The real question is who are these people?"

They were scrutinizing the script, character by character.

"They have a lightning bolt over their heads, unlike the other humans."

"That's easy," said Perry, "They are special in some way. Kings, or shamans, or maybe gods."

"That means there is a relationship between the objects represented by the writing, by the characters. "I'm going to construct a probabilistic network using Bayes Theorem.

Gimme a pencil and some paper, and I will outline it for you."

"For events A and B, provided that $P(B) \neq 0$,
The formula is:
$$P(A|B) = \quad P(A) \, P(B|A)P(B)$$

Which tells us how often A happens, given that B happens (written $P(A|B)$,
when we know how often B happens given that A happens (written $P(B|A)$
and how likely A is on its own, written $P(A)$ and how likely B is on its own, written $P(B)$."

"Let us say $P(Fire)$ means how often there is fire, and $P(Smoke)$ means how often we see smoke, then:
$P(Fire|Smoke)$ means how often there is fire when we can see smoke
$P(Smoke|Fire)$ means how often we can see smoke when there is fire;
So the formula kind of tells us 'forwards' $P(Fire|Smoke)$ when we know 'backwards' $P(Smoke|Fire)$.

Are you following me?" Henry said.

Perry looked at Henry with a puzzled expression. He stuffed more gum into his mouth and began chewing furiously.

"A Bayes net is a model. It reflects the states of some part of a world that is being modeled and it describes how those states are related by probabilities. This model might be of your house, or your classes at school, your body, your community, an ecosystem; anything!

All the possible states of the model represent all the possible scenarios that can exist, that is, all the possible ways that the parts or states can be configured.

The car engine can be running normally or having trouble. Your test results are good, or they suck. Your body can be sick or healthy, and so on.

So where do the probabilities come in?

Well, typically some states will tend to occur more frequently when other states are present.

Thus, if you are sick, the chances of a running nose are higher. If it is cloudy, the chances of rain are higher, and so on.

Here is a simple Bayes net that illustrates these concepts."

Henry drew three ovals, connected by lines. One he labeled 'weather', one he labeled 'sprinkler', and one he labeled 'lawn'.

"Let us say the weather can have three states: sunny, cloudy, or rainy, also that the grass can be wet or dry, and that the sprinkler can be on or off.

Now there are some *causal* links in this relationship, between these three factors. If it is rainy, then it will make the grass wet directly. But if it is sunny for a long time, that too can make the grass wet, indirectly, by causing someone to turn on the sprinkler."

"When actual probabilities are entered into this net that reflect the reality of real weather, lawn, and sprinkler use, such a net can be made to answer a number of useful questions, like, "if the lawn is wet, what are the chances it was caused by rain or by the sprinkler", and "if the chance of rain increases, how does that affect my having to budget time for watering the lawn".

"Ahh, okay, so what?" Perry was rubbing his forehead.

"For example, consider the character which has lightning bolts over its head; two possible explanations for this are: either it is coming into him from the sky, or it is emerging from him as a radiant energy.
Which is more likely? We can use Bayes' Theorem to compute the posterior probability of each explanation.

Let us assume that one of the explanations will tell us if these mean that humans were given divine powers, or evolved to possess them, as on Atlantis perhaps.

We set up a network of data points using the glyphs or script characters.

Each character in the script will be a node, and each node is a variable which has a weighted relationship to all the other nodes.

That will tell us what the unknown characters probably mean. That's why it's called a 'probability' graph."

"Gee, Henry, I'm not sure I've got this," Perry said.

"Don't worry. If nothing else, it will give us more information to work with. Sooner or later, Perry, we're going to crack this code!"

All that night, and most of the next day, the boys huddled together in their room, coming out to steal cookies or glasses of milk, and then—like little mice—sneak back into their hidey-hole.

"Okay, Perry. Here's what I can say with confidence: this tablet is a record, perhaps an *official* record. It describes the power of the king, or god, or whatever that figure is, and how that person is to be regarded by the other social classes.

Actually, it's a typical scenario in history. The king or pharaoh is lord of the land and its inhabitants. He (or she) collects taxes, expects loyalty and obedience, and in return, gives protection and citizenship to his or her people."

"That's just how government works, isn't it, Henry? Only in America, democracy changed the rules so kings don't get to dominate the people; this is an anomaly in politics, and a result of having an educated population who are free to speak and make decisions for themselves."

Henry replied: "Well, that was not the case in this civilization; whoever wrote this record was definitely telling people to obey the leader. Look at this one, and *this* one."

Henry pointed to other characters that appeared to be items of power, like a rod or cane, or maybe a spear. Only the king figure held one. Many of the human figures were kneeling on one knee to the king.

"So do we know enough to be able to translate this into English?" said Perry.

"I think so. Closely enough to have a rough idea." Henry closed his laptop.

"Because if we get a chance to get one more dive in before our parents take us home to Brackendale, we might see some inscriptions that tell us more." Perry's tone was hopeful.

"Let's work on that, send our results to Dr. Wegener at Cornell, and see if he has any further ideas," said Henry.

"Right. That's exactly what we'll do." said Perry.

"I'm starving," Henry remarked. "We didn't eat all day!"

Perry fell to the floor, holding his throat like he was dying or something. He croaked: "Food! Food!"

They laughed as they swung open the door of their little sanctuary of scientific research, and greeted the parents.

"Dad? I have a big favor to ask," Perry began.

"What's that, Perry?"

"I need to dive one last time in the area we got stranded. You know? Like Gilligan's Island?"

"We could. If the boat rental will ever talk to me again!" His Dad was speaking but his mother was giving his father a dirty look.

"How long will we be gone, son?" Mr. Normal was asking.

"I really have to check something, Dad. I will need a full hour on the bottom."

"OK, let me call the rental now."

"Can Henry come?"

"Of course he can. He's like a second son to us."

"Cool! I'll call him once you give me a time."

Thursday was the day. They could have a smaller boat for up to three hours, including leaving and returning to port.

They had fine weather and a calm sea.

Perry's Mom prepared a generous lunch, and Henry's Mom added a soup she made using her own mother's recipe. It was a fish chowder: healthy and tasty.

"Bring me back a shell, " said Gabby, kissing Perry on the cheek. "And don't take chances. When you are tired, just come up, okay?"

"Okay, Sis," Perry replied.

He was grateful for a sister, who was always watching out for him. Maybe that's why his family kind of adopted Henry since Henry himself had no brothers or sisters.

With a full tank of gas, and the newest electronic instruments, Robert Normal followed his previous route out past the docks and piers and luxury yachts and fishing boats with their battered pride—out to the endless emptiness of blue.

This time he plotted a course slightly south, aimed directly at the cays of North Bahamas.
This seemed to be the place, thought Perry. *I am over the ancient ruins of a great city, a city lost in legend and Time.*

The boys donned their wetsuits and tanks, and were over the side in no time.

Henry's fancy diving watch had a number of features, one of which was a GPS locator that he had only learned about recently. He had the coordinates dialed in, making it much easier to navigate underwater.

Underwater, every rock and boulder, every ledge and drop-off looked the same. They had encrustations of sponge and coral, sea anemones, little colonies of crustaceans that were quite familiar, but no help in determining where you were, or where you should be.

'Technology' Henry's dad Peter had said, when he gave his son this expensive watch for his birthday. Indeed. This technology would have saved Columbus a lot of uncertain sailing, and perhaps would have helped him realize there was no way to find India from the Caribbean.

The boys backpedalled with their long yellow fins, as they surveyed the seafloor over a hundred square yard area, nearly the size of a football field.

Perry signaled and Henry followed.

The columns and trilithons emerge out of the dim distance, and this time Perry could see a bit more.

Henry's watch pinged--indicating they had the correct GPS position as compared to last time, the time the Bermuda Triangle showed them its teeth.

Henry wasn't sure what to look for, so he took tons of pictures from different angles, and poked about down in the chaotic ruins of a once-great monument to the greatness of Humanity.

Perry was following a line of pavement stones, quite similar to the Bimini Road, that led to an enormous edifice that towered from quite a deep place down in the shadows, right up to almost the surface.

He knew that entryways are important, and often have symbols or inscriptions to tell about what this place is and what it is for.

This one was surely important; it was of large size and scale compared to the other structures on the site.

What made Perry's heart beat much faster was two things he noticed only as he came up close to the doorway.
One, there was the now-familiar script, the hieroglyphs of men and super-men, the ones with lightning bolts going into the top of their heads.

"Why is it going in, not coming out, Perry?" Henry had asked.

"That must mean this power comes from God, or Heaven, or maybe aliens," Perry had stated. "It means it does not come from *them!*"

One of the lightning bolts was larger, and it zapped a figure that was also larger than the regular glyphs for human beings.

The other thing Perry noticed is that the letters, the symbols, were inlaid with gold or some metal that shone like gold.

Orichalcum! Perry had learned in his reading that a rare alloy of gold and silver, perhaps with a trace of copper called 'orichalcum' was used exclusively on Atlantis.

Their technology was superior to ours, so it made sense that their metallurgy was also beyond anything we had developed ourselves.

Humanity--history teaches-- went from the Stone Age of stone and bone tools to the age of metals: first the Bronze Age and later the Iron Age.

It was the smelting of iron, and its derivative, steel, that changed the world of old to a modern world of industry and manufacture.

Precious metals are used for adornment, and highly valued. But the metaphysical properties of such metals--and the related knowledge--was lost centuries ago.

Perry had memorized the meaning of the symbols, about twenty of them. The one that was not on the tablets was a volcano and here was clearly a volcano.

Here--over the entrance to the Great Hall--was the symbol—a smoking mountain. But it did not have a metal inlay, and appeared to be hastily carved or chipped out at the last minute.
Perry read the rest of it.
   Here ruled the wise kings (gods?) of Atlantis, and here are their tombs.

It was a tomb. Or at least partially.

There was an inner passage, with a tunnel leading downward.

Some unearthly light illuminated the first ten yards then it turned and twisted out of sight.

Somewhere down there in the darkness of ten thousand years, lay the secrets of the kings of Atlantis!

   I have found it! I have found Atlantis. That is what the symbol of the temple with a double crown and single star over its roof meant!

The kingdom! Atlantis the Mighty! Home of the Gods of Antiquity! Home of Poseidon, the God of the Sea!

Wait till I tell Henry! Wait! Where is Henry?

For one brief, heart-stopping moment, Perry had realized that he left Henry alone, over in the main complex, by himself. Just like he had found Gabby, also alone.

I'm so stupid. I'm so sorry, Henry. If anything has happened to you, I'll never forgive myself.

But Henry was just fine, still snapping pictures of his adventure of a lifetime.

Perry swam swiftly over to him, grabbed his arm, and pointed upwards.

What Perry did not observe, however was a shadowy figure hovering behind a statue of Poseidon, holding his breath so his bubbles could not be seen.

***

"Dad!" Perry said with his first breath of fresh air in over an hour.
"You won't believe what I found!"

Perry recounted his own marvelous experience, which belonged to him alone, alone with the proof that he so desperately wanted to have.

"I knew we could do it," said Henry, matter-of-factly, like it was easy as pie.

"I'm so proud of you son, and of you too, Henry! You did what many others have tried to do, and have not been successful. We're going to make sure the world hears about this.

Henry, you have the photographic evidence, and Perry—you have the tablets. We can carbon-date them, or use the new technology of uranium-dating, to show their age.

I'll talk to my lawyer and see whether we have to surrender them to the State of Florida, or we can satisfy the federal law by donating them to a museum much closer to home: the Brackendale Museum of Natural History."

Robert turned the boat toward port, and inside of an hour, they were back, safe and sound.

"Mom! We're okay!" Perry's cell was back up.

"Oh, thank goodness! Gabby and I were waiting on the edge of our chairs! Tell your father to pick up takeout on the way back."

Dusk had come to the beaches and coast of Florida.

But far offshore, seventy feet down, near a ruined temple, a bright spotlight was switched on, and a lone diver entered through the gateway, hardly noticing the letters with the metal script inlaid by an ancient craftsman so long ago.

Perhaps he didn't care. He had a mission to fulfill.

Chapter Fourteen Where Angels Fear To Tread

The solo diver had come equipped with an extra tank of air, floodlights with large batteries, and a metal detector. He was ducking down here and there, as if looking for something.

He would often stop, and swing the boom of the detector back and forth, back and forth, sweeping the landscape with a practiced hand.

There was no one else there.

There was a celebration of sorts at the hotel, when Perry's news was shared with the parents. Peter had wanted to thank the Normal family for taking such good care of Henry, so he arranged a buffet dinner at a local seafood restaurant.

Henry was filling up not one, not two,—but *three* plates at once, with lobster tail, deep-fried shrimps, poached kingfish—which turned out to be a mackerel, known for being tender and tasty.

Perry and Gabby were close behind.

The parents were enjoying a bottle of champagne, and the waiter was lighting the candles on all the tables.

The underwater world at night is like the night on shore--different animals come out to do their hunting. In Miami it was thugs and thieves, clubbers and party animals.

Beyond the reef among the hundreds of islands and sandbars sharks patrolled, jellyfish lit up with phosphorescence drifted with the tides, and other creatures continued their relentless quest for food or mates.

The human diver-- with his own hunting style-- was probing further and further into the Great Hall of the Kings of Atlantis.
He didn't *know* that, of course, but he suspected it.

There must be vast wealth here, he told himself.
Why had Perry returned again and again to these waters to search?
He knew the boy was very clever, and he knew the boy had come to Florida for a reason, had learned to dive in deep water because he was looking for treasure too.

"Are you kidding, Henry? Dessert? How can you think of that, after eating five plates of seafood and salad?"

"I can't have dinner without dessert, Perry. Something sweet and gooshy, like pumpkin pie with whipped cream, or creme caramel, or Black Forest cake with a ton of icing."

"Well, why *not?*" said Perry.

"Because you'll wind up a fat slug when you are forty," said Gabby.

Girls were always watching their diet, watching the calories for every bite, Henry thought to himself. *I'm a guy—I burn it all off!*

***

The mouth of the tunnel summoned the lone diver. He dropped his tank onto the sand, and holding his breath, switched to the reserve tank. His metal detector was left behind.

He entered the tunnel with his lights switched off-- the very stones of the walls and ceiling seemed to glow pale green, leading him down, down, down into the deeps.

Like a moth attracted to a candle flame, Darius Frame was drawn to meet his fate at last.

***

The newspaper on Saturday reported that a boat had been washed up on shore up north near Boca Raton.
It took them until Monday to trace the serial number painted on each side of the bow.
The boat was registered to Key Largo Dive Club.

But whoever had skippered the motorboat was nowhere to be found.

"Hey people," said Gabby, reading, after breakfast on the balcony.
"Isn't that the dive school where you trained, Perry?"
"Key Largo? Yes. That is Darius Frame's school."
"Well, not anymore. He's been lost at sea."

"You're kidding, right?" said Perry.

But Gabby was not kidding; it said right there, and had a picture of the dive boat that was so familiar to Perry, and Henry.

The dive boat that had started their adventure, and had led to friendship with other novice divers like Santiago and Amy and even led them to Tareq-- in a way.

"I wonder what happened to Tareq?" Perry was saying.

"You mean, after he lost the debate to my little brother?" said Gabby cattily.

"I feel bad for Darius," Perry said in a soft voice.

"The guy who almost had both of us killed out there in the savage waters of the ocean? Not me! I'm not happy that he's dead, but I'm not sorry either!"
Gabby was still upset, that much was clear.

Perry turned inward, perhaps to say a prayer for a man whose only sin was to be greedy, which made him willing to use others to get what he wanted.

Not so different from any other treasure-hunter really.

Chapter Fifteen   The Legend Lives On

"I think we have an excellent case, Henry. But honestly, I think we will have to wait for other evidence that will convince a doubting world that Atlantis was real."

Perry was munching on an apple.
His suitcases were packed, and the flight was in two hours.

"Could we go bother Professor Wegener again? He might have an idea how we follow up on our efforts here in Florida."

"I suppose we could, Henry. And don't forget—there's Mr. Bob Caygeon who is curator at the Brackendale Museum of American History in town.
He's someone we have never had a chance to talk to, and I'll bet he knows quite a bit," Perry said.
I'll bet he's even heard of Atlantis!"

"Perry? Henry?" Perry's Mom came in the room.

"All packed honey? Henry, I think your parents are wanting you to get ready. We'll have you over for dinner later in the week. We can do a slideshow of all your photographs. Sound good?"

"Oh, sure, Mrs. Normal. I think that's a great idea!"

Perry, Gabby, and the Normals were on a flight just behind the one taking Henry and his parents home. It was a direct flight to Rochester, where they had parked the SUV only a few weeks earlier, although it seemed like months!

Perry missed his gang of friends who hang out at The Malt Shop. He had some much to tell them! He was sure they had stories about camp, or summer adventures of their own.

The end of August was always a sweet time of reunion for middle-schoolers. Living in a small, cozy town like Brackendale was like living in a dream.

Perry got in touch with the professor on Skype.

"Yes, yes, my boy, I have your correspondence. Very interesting, very interesting."

The professor had a habit of repeating everything twice. Maybe it was his way of expressing his thoughts, considering he spent many years in his own head mulling over theories and methodologies.

"Sir? Where do we go from here?" Perry was curious.

"Well, Perry, if you were one of my students, you would write a peer-reviewed paper in some scientific or historical journal.

Given that you are only a 7th-grader, I recommend that you keep an accurate record of what you did, what you found, and when you get to university, consider expanding your research in a scholarly way."

"I would like to go down to Bimini again someday. Would the university sponsor me to do more research?"

"There is always funding available for bright young students like yourself, Perry.

And let me say this: I think you were very brave to do all the things you did: learned to scuba dive, spend significant amounts of your vacation exploring underwater, at some personal risk—as you know—all in the name of seeking the truth about a legendary lost culture that may have shaped American history in ways we cannot imagine."

"Adventure is my middle name, sir!"

"Yes, Perry, yes it is. I know you are quite well known in upstate New York now. One day, no doubt, the world will know who you are. Good luck to you, Perry!"

"Thank you, Professor Wegener. And, oh, about the time travel episodes I told you about earlier in the year?

They really *did* happen! Goodbye, professor."

***

"Oh Perry, Henry? Come here for a second."

Perry's Mom and Henry's Mom were in the kitchen preparing a large meal for the families. Even Gabby was making salad. Gabby never cooked at all!

"What is it, Dad?" said Perry.

"*The New York Times* has an article here about your friend Tareq that I thought you might find interesting."

"Henry! Look! It's him! He wrote an article about the mystery underwater city near Cuba. But he's not calling it 'mystery city'—he's claiming it is lost Atlantis! Oh. My. Gawd."

Henry, Perry, and Robert Normal were huddled around the laptop--all trying to read what the world-famous newspaper said.
A young scholar from Florida State claims to have definitive evidence that the lost city of Atlantis

was real, and it has been found in the Gulf of
Mexico.

"What a joke!" said Henry. "He argued and denied any possibility that Atlantis ever existed, and now he's saying 'Oh, *no*—it's *real!*"

The newspaper article online went on to give details that the boys were already aware of, especially since Perry had used this fact to defeat Tareq at the Broward College debate only weeks before.

"Let him have it," said Perry. "It only confirms that we were right, and that proof of Atlantis in our part of the world is lying right there on the seabed, right under our noses—if we would only look!"

"But he took the credit for it, Perry! That's cheating! That's totally unfair!"

"Not entirely, my boy. Remember—all those people, including the local media—heard us speak, saw our presentation; they are witnesses to who really broke the news. If we want to push it, I can get confirmation of that from the Florida papers.
But really, he's on our side now, Henry. Think about it."

Perry leaned back into the sofa with a big smile on his face.

Henry was about to say something, but the ladies called 'Dinner!' which was a much more important event, from Henry's point of view, at this precise moment.

"To Perry and Henry," said Robert Normal, raising his glass of wine.

"To Perry and Henry!" repeated everyone in a hearty voice. "Cheers!"

It had been a real adventure alright, the boys were thinking.

"By the way, I sent an e-mail to Tareq, congratulating him on his 'discovery' and on his bold assertion that it is the missing civilization. I wished him 'all the best' in his further work on determining who built that marvel of an underwater city."

"That's good, Perry," said Peter, Henry's Dad. "That shows maturity, instead of petty jealousy. This is how Science builds on itself—new discoveries, new investigation. New findings. Cheers!"

Since the Schuylers liked good wine, and the Normals were happy to drink the bottle that their friends had brought, everyone was toasting and smiling like it was a holiday or something.

Perhaps the biggest smile was on the faces of the two intrepid voyagers who had gone well beyond their limitations, and accomplished something of real value to history.

Epilogue

As things turned out, Mr. Bob Caygeon of the Brackendale Museum of American History was delighted to receive the precious artifacts that Perry and Henry had retrieved on their Florida adventure.

He was actually amazed at the tablets, the photographs--the whole account of how they came into the possession of two local boys.

The *Brackendale Courier* sent a reporter to cover the story, and take pictures of the two heroes.

Everybody in town would now hear the tale. People love it when their own neighbors and local citizens do something great. There would be more glasses lifted in recognition of what they had done, in every home and tavern in town.

There was one last thing for Perry to do.

He needed to write a letter.

August 17, 2017

Office of Archaeological Resource Protection,
Dept. of the Interior, Bureau of Reclamation,
Washington, D.C. 20240

To Whom It May Concern

This is to notify you that certain artifacts of archaeological value and significance have been retrieved by me in local and international waters off Florida. As required by law, I certify that all such artifacts have been declared in this document (see Appendix).

All artifacts and objects retrieved have been placed into the care and custody of the Brackendale Museum of American History, in Brackendale, N.Y., as authentic relics of early American history.

The museum curator, Mr. Bob Caygeon, has accepted said artifacts, and agreed to be custodian of them on behalf of the United States Government, until such time as the federal authority releases them, or physically claims them.

Please direct all questions concerning this matter to me at the address below.

Perry Normal
9 Galileo Court
Brackendale, New York 14519.
USA

With thanks,

Perry

Read <u>all</u> the Perry Normal Adventure Series!

Look for them in paperback and Kindle editions at Amazon.com under "Perry Normal Adventures", or at Indigo.ca.

Inquire about other titles and purchase through:

myredpine@gmail.com

Follow author Mason Stone at his blog:
http://perryisnormal.blogspot.ca